VAMPIRES OF A CERTAIN AGE

FIVE HUNDRED YEARS OF LOVING

STELLA FOSSE

COVER

DIANA ROSINUS

ISBN: 978-1-950227-09-9

Cover by Diana Rosinus (https://www.dianarosinus.com/)

Published by:

Baubo Books

125 S Estes Drive #4311,

Chapel Hill, NC 27514, USA

www.stellafosse.com

CONTENTS

I am and not, I freeze and yet am burned,
Since from myself another self I turned.

Let me live with some more sweet content,
Or die and so forget what love ere meant.

—Queen Elizabeth I

PROLOGUE

YORKSHIRE, ENGLAND, 1544

Marion smelled the wolf and the wolf could smell her. He rattled the door against the latch, as she sat with her back against the rough oak to keep him out. And he, on the other side, snuffled through the gap between door and frame, with his ragged breath and his hunger. Her body was a better prize than the vermin in the woods, if only he could reach her.

In front of Marion a single candle burned on an oak table draped with mint and verbena and sage, materials of her trade. Every remedy she made she tested on herself before she gave it to the villagers, with the exception of the deadliest mixtures, which she neither tested nor sold. Some in the village came to her, desperate, and asked for such things, the permanent cure for a bleak life or a violent husband, but Marion told them she did not keep such tinctures. Of course that was a lie. There was one vial on the topmost shelf, waiting for extreme need. As the hours passed with the wolf still outside, Marion began to nod, so tired, and half-dreamed of feeding that deadly potion to the wolf; but no, he would eat her first.

The shutters were closed and barred for the night, so she could neither see nor hear what the wolf perceived across the clearing. She only knew that at some point in their grim visit, as she drifted in and out of exhausted sleep, the wolf grew distracted. The rough breath through the doorframe hesitated, stopped, and he was gone. But why?

Then she heard voices through the woods, and then closer. Despite the glow of the candle, a faint outline of light grew bright around the edge of the shutters. Now the sounds were louder: the angry shouts of a mob. A fate worse than the wolf approached. The men of the village had come for her at last.

CHAPTER ONE

There were days when Marion longed for the sixteenth century, witch trials and open sewers notwithstanding. But here she was, trapped in the age of fast food, as her new employee Amber Pettis unwrapped a cheeseburger. The scent of carrion wafted across her desk.

"Sorry to eat in your office, Marion. Noon was the only time we could meet. Here," Amber waved a French fry. "I have lots. Want some?"

Marion shook her head. "No, thank you. I'm not hungry."

"Are you ever?"

Marion arched one eyebrow. "I beg your pardon."

"Seriously, I have never seen you take one bite of food." Amber lifted the sandwich to her mouth. The dripping catsup was a nice deep red. The rest of the meal looked fake, like paper mâché food.

Amber chewed with gusto, then swallowed. "Are you on some diet?"

"You could say that."

"How long have you been on it?"

"About five hundred years."

Amber giggled and covered her mouth with her napkin. "I'll bet it feels like that."

"It does." Marion toyed with telling Amber who she really was, a mistake she made with a mortal every century or so. Although the fact that her blood bank did not have a single window might have been a clue.

"So… what do you eat?"

"It's a liquid diet, really."

Amber laughed. "Remember when people used to say, 'I'm on a liquid diet,' and meant they only drank booze?" She stopped laughing. "You're not an alcoholic, are you?"

"Not even close."

"Well then, what?" Amber paused. With any luck she had just remembered she was talking with the blood bank president. But Amber continued undaunted. "Oh—am I being insensitive? Is it a medical condition?"

"Yes, it is medical, actually. I don't mind you asking. But if I explained you might be offended."

"Is it a religious thing? Because, you know, I'm not religious. But I don't mind if other people are."

Marion smiled. "In a way. I am sure I believe in things that you don't."

"Now, that's intriguing." Amber crumpled her empty food wrappers. Her phone pinged. She checked a text. "We'll talk more later. The mobile collection units just pulled in, and my team is gearing up for testing."

"Of course."

Amber turned on her way out. "Let's go out for drinks."

"I don't drink alcohol."

"Well then what do you—oh never mind." Amber tossed her wrappers in the bin and was out the door.

Marion could hear Vivienne's voice as clearly as if her friend from long ago were in the room.

"You cannot tell them. They do not understand our life, and so they despise us. To them we are at best parasites, at worst an abomination. Don't make them

hate you. Keep your secret to yourself."

Marion kept her counsel, but Amber's curiosity was growing. Marion had hired Amber to run the quality department, and curiosity was essential to find and fix problems. But the company president's feeding habits were well outside Amber's purview. Even so, Marion felt Amber's eyes on her, especially at lunchtime. Marion could not even pretend to eat what a mortal would consider a meal.

The holidays arrived, and with them invitations to parties, those festivals of consumption. Marion made the usual excuses: she had a conflict, she felt unwell, she had to work that evening. But she could not beg off hosting the year-end party at her own blood bank. The staff gathered in a glassed-in conference room at the center of the building. Just beyond the windows were impressive blood testing machines. Behind the machines, lined up against the walls, banks of refrigerators stored blood that made Marion hungry for real food, not this steak-and-potatoes nonsense on her plate.

Once the caterers cleared the dishes, Marion rose to welcome their featured speaker. Mark Jameson, head of the Midwestern Blood Bank Association, stood and raised his glass. "It's been a year," he said, to low murmurs of agreement. "And by that I mean, it's been a year of challenges. Of belt tightening. Of exciting advances in our field, yet lower demand for our products. A smaller market for blood is a good thing for the human race—although not for us."

Marion resumed her seat as he continued. Most blood was fractionated now, divided into its component parts: Red cells for trauma, plasma for burns, platelets for clotting. That made blood go farther, which staved off shortages but meant less demand. *Except from vampires,* she thought. Vampires seldom died, and every so often, one vampire created another. If every blood bank catered to vampires and not just mortals, business would boom. Marion had a mad impulse to raise her hand and suggest a new business model.

"Marion!" Amber stage-whispered from across the table. "What are you thinking? You look amused. This speech isn't funny."

"Sorry, Amber, I'll try to concentrate."

Jameson continued with statistics on everything: State-wide blood use. Their sales. Their costs. Their profit margins. Not for the first time, Marion grew nostalgic for the days when blood was blood and marketing meant some guy wearing a sandwich board.

When the event was over, Marion shook the speaker's hand. "Thanks for your comments, Mark. We're so focused on the day-to-day. It's great to hear your broader perspective."

"Glad to be here, Marion. You're looking well. When was the last time we ran into each other? Four, five years ago? You look exactly the same."

Marion said goodnight and made a mental note to add more gray highlights to her hair. Trying to look older was a bother. She headed for the parking lot, where Amber caught up with her. "You didn't eat. Again. You just pushed the food around your plate."

"Hmm." Why was playing mortal so tiresome?

"Marion. Are you going to tell me what's going on? You aren't sick, are you?"

She smiled. "No. Never better."

"Well then what is it? Come over to my house and talk to me."

Marion gave in to the inevitable.

Amber lived in a condo by a lake. It was clean and neat and worth a fortune these days. After centuries of investing, Marion could have bought the whole complex without batting an eye.

Amber welcomed Marion to her home and gestured to the couch in the living room. "Sit. Have a glass of—no, you won't have wine, will you?"

"No thanks."

Amber perched on one arm of the couch, a glass of ruby red wine in her hand. "So. Why don't you eat? Or drink?"

"You won't let this go, will you?"

"Nope."

Marion sighed. "Oh, alright. I drink blood."

Amber stared at her for a second and then burst out laughing. "Sure you do."

Marion didn't laugh. "I can't believe I said that."

"Because it's baloney."

"No; it's true. But I know better than to say it."

Amber stopped laughing. "So when you said you'd been on this diet for five hundred years—"

"I wasn't exaggerating."

"Are you telling me you're a—"

"Vampire. The word you want is vampire."

"Oh come on. You're yanking my chain."

"No. I'm not."

"Alright. Tell me—"

"How I came to be one?"

"No. How your immune system works. As a dead person."

Marion laughed. "That's a new one."

"I'm serious. If you're 'undead,' or whatever you call it, how do you fight off disease?" Amber sipped her wine. "Inquiring minds want to know."

"I have no idea. I've had other fish to fry this last half millennium."

"Like what?"

"Like surviving. And helping others of my kind survive."

"Surviving. As a vampire."

"Yes."

"Alright, I'll bite." Amber laughed at her accidental joke. "How, exactly, did you become a vampire?"

Marion stared at nothing. "It's hard to remember that far back. But I know that my house was on fire."

CHAPTER TWO

Marion stood and closed one eye to look out through the edges of the shutters. She saw their faces in the torchlight, dimly, as they crossed the clearing: men who had come to her secretly for years, one by one, searching for courage or virility, searching for fertility, searching to make some woman love them and redeem their empty existence. They would never admit they relied on her; the other men of the pack would have shunned them or worse.

Me, the one who healed them and their children, she thought. *Me, the one to whom they told their secrets, their fears and desires. Who will cure their children if they burn me tonight? Do they think on that?*

No. And the bar across the door would not stop them. Even sitting against the door would be no match for the mob. If they could not get to her they would set their torches to the thatched roof of Marion's cottage. But she would not let them kill her. Marion climbed atop the rough wood bench to reach the deadly dusty bottle she had saved all these years. She would do the job herself.

It had been a good life, a fine life. She had enjoyed almost all of it. She raised the poisoned vial in a toast to life and then drank, as the men pounded on the door and demanded entrance. Her last thought was to wish the wolf would devour them all, one by one. She was still conscious as she fell, sure she would be dead before she hit the floor.

"Damn you, Marion, why did you do that?" Strong womanly arms caught her in midair and drew her close. The pounding on the door and the beating of her heart were one, and then there was only the pounding, and then nothing.

Marion was unaware when strong arms carried her out the back cottage window and into the woods. She was still unconscious when strong jaws gripped her throat, bore down on an artery, sucked out poison along with her blood. The woman in black groaned, not from the pleasure of feeding, but from the force of the poison on her system. And when it was done, when Marion's savior could not take in one more drop, she pulled back her sleeve, bit her own wrist and tore her own artery. She pressed the wound roughly against Marion's slack lips, as a farmer might press a newborn lamb's mouth to the teat of its mother.

In a moment Marion responded. Still unconscious, she drank unknowing from the other's wrist, drank the blood of centuries, blood that had travelled from mother vampire to daughter vampire long before this benighted century.

Marion awoke still cradled by her rescuer. They were in the woods behind the cottage. How had they escaped? She could not remember. But she had to know. "How did..."

"Shh!" the woman whispered. "Don't let on that we're here. Let them think they've burnt you."

When Marion looked past her companion's face, nothing was the same. The sky was no longer black, but a deep blue purple. The stars were bursts of color, somehow closer than before. She could smell the men in the clearing, the burning tar of their torches, the sweat on their foreheads. And each man had his own scent: The butcher smelled of blood and ale; the priest smelled of wax and wool stained with ancient sweat. Their voices, no longer one swelling mob, sounded now like a chorus with distinct parts: the treble of tenors and the low burr of basses. And behind the mob were all the scents of the forest: oaks and elms and plane trees, every kind with its own distinct aroma. Marion could almost place the scent of each particular tree. It was overwhelming, as if the whole world were made anew.

Enchanted by what she saw, Marion rose and stepped away from the sheltering bush. She was standing, listening and sniffing the air, when the strange woman whispered to her.

"Come back!" she hissed. "One of them is looking our way!"

The men had set fire to the cottage thatch, and by the glow of the flames, Marion saw that her companion was a solid woman all in black. The woman carried herself like a swordfighter, had big arms and strong legs. Yet that impressive physical presence did not begin to hint at the speed and strength that had saved Marion from the mob.

Nausea found Marion and she retched, turning to spare her rescuer. The sound caught someone's attention.

"Oh Hell," said the woman in black, as one of the torch bearers split from the crowd of revelers and came toward them.

It was Jack, a young man who lived at the closest edge of the village. Jack, whose daughters Marion had delivered. Jack, whose manhood Marion had restored with a potion. He approached the undergrowth where they hid, torch held high, his expression curious, and peered around the edge of the bush.

Marion's companion spoke to him in soft insistent tones. "If you make a sound I will drain your blood until you are dead. Hie thee back to the others, silently, and say nothing of what you have seen, not ever in your life. You will maintain forever that this witch died in the burning of her cottage. Nod to show that you agree, and I will spare you."

Jack nodded, looking dazed, and returned to the group. The strange woman said, "That should hold him for a while, at least until we are gone. It would be a waste to kill them all. And as for you, have you finished retching?"

"Yes," said Marion. She wanted to know how it was that she was alive. But she did not ask, not yet.

"Good." The woman stood. "Now let us be off. We must be to York before the sun."

As they walked away, Marion looked back and saw the men in the clearing dancing the dance of conquerors. *Death to all witches*, they crowed. Of course they never found her body; yet they would pretend to each other that they had burned the cottage with her inside. But some in the village would die without medicine in the winter ahead.

Her benefactor led Marion to a clearing where a horse grazed, tied to a branch. Once they were on its back and walking away, Marion ventured to speak.

"That draught should have killed me," said Marion.

The other woman laughed. "It did. Welcome to eternal life."

"Eternal life is promised by Our Lord and Savior only to those who pass through the gates of Heaven."

"Heaven is a place on earth. A place where witches save each other."

"I am no witch!"

"You are now. You heard them say so."

"Those men are ignorant. I am a healer."

"Indeed. They condemned their physician, and in doing so condemned themselves."

"Who are you?"

"I have taken the name Vivienne. We go now to York, where women such as us find ways to hide. You will learn our ways. And when the time comes, you will save others like you and me, women condemned to die for their good works. The world will not always exist in darkness. Someday we will not only be tolerated but celebrated. It has happened before and will happen again."

Marion shook her head. "Methinks such a time is many years away."

"And now you have received the gift of many years and you will live to see it. And perhaps you will see a dark time again, and another enlightened time. All things have their season and their circuit, as the earth circles the sun."

"The earth circles the sun? You speak blasphemy."

"'Tis not blasphemy. 'Tis natural philosophy. I had it from the astronomer Rheticus, whose teacher Copernicus has known it for years. Rheticus finally convinced his mentor to publish what he learned." Vivienne lowered her voice, though there was none but Marion to hear. "Rheticus is a night-dweller, you see. Star gazing is a fine calling for those who are awake by night." They rode on through dark forest by the purple light of the circling stars.

On the night the men invaded her clearing, torches in hand, Marion Chase was nearing forty years old—longer than the lifespan of most women of that time. She wore long skirts and a laced up bodice, in the custom of the day. Her hair was wavy and black, with lines of silver just beginning. Her hands were stained green and brown from her work with concoctions. Strong hands, a woman's hands. But her strength had limits, until now. As their horse walked under a tree with a thick, low-hanging branch, Marion, unthinking, broke off the branch with one hand and wondered at her new strength.

Through the long night Marion and her companion rode beside the River Nidd, heading southeast toward York with the moon above them. Once, Marion, exhausted, began to nod off.

"Stay alert, now. Plenty of time to sleep in the day."

"Why would I sleep then?"

"I shall tell you. But first I must ask: Who among those men spurred them to turn on you?"

"It was no man who set them on me. It was a woman."

"A woman who loved you? Or a woman who hated you?"

"Indeed, there was one of each. They are sisters."

"And that, Amber, is how I was bloodborn." Marion looked up and was not surprised by the slack-mouthed look of shock on Amber's face. "And now I suppose you'll turn in your resignation? But you did ask, you know."

Amber shook herself and focused. "You're right. I was desperate to know why you didn't eat. Now I know. And now I have a million questions. Like, why exactly does a vampire want to run a blood bank?"

"A fine question." Marion stood. "But that was enough for one night. More answers must wait for another day."

"Alright. Goodnight, Boss. And thank you for an illuminating evening. More fun tomorrow."

If you show up, thought Marion. But she just waved goodnight.

LAKE COUNTY BLOOD BANK, 2024

CHAPTER THREE

Amber walked proudly into the blood bank on her fifth anniversary as Vice President of Quality. She had weathered many a storm, including learning about her boss' true nature. That night had been a shock, for sure. But there was something about Amber's misspent youth that helped her regain her equilibrium. Hidden away in her closet were photos of high school Amber with black lipstick and her hair dyed black, with one pierced eyebrow and pale makeup. If she had not spent her college years as a vampire wannabe, listening to *The Horrors* and watching *Twilight* reruns, she probably would have quit on the spot. And she remembered the day when Marion finally explained the hidden second business the blood bank conducted.

"Tell me, Amber: All that blood we reject because it carries human disease. All that blood we can't sell because it expired like last week's milk. What do we do with it?"

Amber knew the answer cold. "We send it to a licensed destruction facility, just like the FDA regulations tell us."

"No, Amber, we do not. Not at this blood bank. There are people out there who need that blood—immortals who aren't affected by human disease. Who can feed on blood when it's infected, or when it's almost too old to help mortals. We feed the immortals, and they in turn have no need to feed on the innocent."

That had been another shock, no doubt about it. But on reflection, Amber had decided that providing Midwestern vampires with discarded blood was better than unleashing them on the citizenry. And so here she was, a leader in the community, second in command at the biggest blood bank in Chicagoland.

Highland Park was a Chicago bedroom community with beaches on the lake, several Frank Lloyd Wright homes, and the feel of a gated community without the gates. The Lake County Blood Bank was housed in a modern single-story building on the outskirts of town. With no windows except the smoked glass entry doors, the place had a bunker-like appearance. Just inside the front doors, a small lobby had a reception desk at the back. Those glass doors were the only exterior glass in the building. To the right of reception was a room where volunteers arrived five mornings a week to donate blood or plasma. In the donation room, big comfortable chairs were arranged in a circle with collection equipment beside each one.

Locked doors to the left of reception led to the testing area, a large room filled with machines the size of large refrigerators where each unit of blood was checked for a dozen diseases that blood can transmit. Blood donors are a healthy bunch. By and large they are careful with their health and free of disease. But the last thing a blood recipient needs is a blood-borne illness, and so blood is carefully tested by trained technicians for diseases ranging from HIV to hepatitis to Zika. Technicians label each blood bag to show when it was drawn, when it expires, the blood type, and the results of all testing. Some blood is used as whole blood, while other blood is separated into components for patients with different needs. All this was done according to protocols written by Amber and her staff.

Blood that tested positive for any disease was stored separately, along with blood that passed its expiration date without being used. That discarded blood was labeled for destruction—but Amber knew its real fate.

The testing room smelled faintly of isopropyl alcohol. The ambient sound was the soft whirring of well-maintained equipment. The machines had the chrome sheen of a high-end coffee cafe. Voices were soft and well-modulated. Technicians wore white lab coats over office casual dress.

The day shift at the blood bank was cheerful and well trained. When there was a tour by visitors or FDA inspectors, the staff smiled and explained the testing they performed. At lunchtime the day shift took their meals to a glassed-in patio behind the building, where they got their dose of sunshine for the day.

The night shift at the blood bank seldom saw visitors. They were good at their jobs but perhaps not quite as cheerful. If pressed, they could explain just as well how they performed the various tests for blood safety. The official demands on their time were lower because there was less blood to process. This was good, because the night shift was busy elsewhere, in a basement of the building that was not on any floorplan. There they performed research on Marion's favorite project: the development of artificial blood to benefit both mortals and immortals. And the technicians prepared discarded blood for another destination: themselves, and others like them.

Their second business, no less important than blood transfusions for the living, was providing ethically sourced blood to the vampires of the Midwest. "We are saving lives here," Marion once told Amber. "Not just vampire lives—human lives. Mortal lives. I'd like to think that if our blood bank went under, every vampire who comes here would only feed on rats and road kill. But I'm not naïve, and you should not be either."

To keep that second business going, they had to keep it a secret—especially from the FDA.

Amber passed Marion's office and saw the blood bank president beckon to her.

"Come in! Congratulations on your anniversary, Amber. Well done. It's been a great five years, so far. We could not do it without you."

"Thanks, Boss. Proud to be here."

Marion gestured. "Here, have a seat. I've been meaning to ask: We're overdue for an FDA inspection. Is everybody ready to go?"

"As of last week, every staff member on both shifts is fully trained and signed off. And they all know the inspection could happen any day —or on the other hand, not for months." Amber smiled. "Too bad the FDA doesn't make an appointment."

Marion rolled her eyes. "Their unpredictability is part of their charm. But we've done a good job up till now, keeping them in line. Let's be sure we do it again."

The FDA inspector and the company president are natural adversaries. They both understand that every organization has flaws. The company president knows where the bodies are buried and wants them to stay that way, while the FDA inspector is intent on digging them up. As president of her blood bank, Marion Chase knew exactly where the bodies were buried—literally. The bodies worked the night shift—a fact that she kept quiet.

The inspection head for the blood bank is in the precarious position of presenting data truthfully, but in the best possible light. That was Amber's role, and she excelled at it. Amber Pettis was in her thirties, ginger haired and pleasantly round, her long hair pulled back and bangs over her hazel eyes. She was just over five feet and disdained heels despite her compact height. Amber loved her job. She loved helping patients all over Chicagoland. She loved knowing the ins and outs of everything that happened at the blood bank. And most of all, she loved working for Marion Chase, who had to be the best mentor any woman could have.

It wasn't just how much Marion knew. Although if there was anything about blood banking that Marion didn't know, it would be news to Amber. Marion understood every part of their business: from logistics to new ways of testing to an unparalleled grasp of the history of what she called "the magic of transferring life from person to person." It was how Marion thought and acted that made her such a great mentor: how she strategized, how she prioritized, how she could walk into a room and mesmerize everyone there. If Amber ever developed half the charisma that woman had, she would be thrilled.

And, too, there was the pay, which was quite generous, and the perks, which were fantastic: everything from tickets to the best shows in town, to jewels at Christmas that were absolutely exquisite. Back when she was new to the blood bank, Amber balked at accepting such gifts, but then she realized there were no strings attached except discretion. Marion just wanted her to do her job and do it well.

"You be my eyes and ears, out there in the sunshine," Marion would tell her. "Go where I can't go. Come back and tell me about these meetings and conferences. And help me run this shop, of course." Marion would smile with pride and a little sadness. "All my dreams are wrapped up in this place. And one of these days I won't be here any longer, and you will carry on."

Amber did not like the sound of that. It wasn't as if Marion needed to retire. She had known Marion for five years now, and her boss had not changed a bit. But that was the point, wasn't it? How long could a woman look exactly the same before someone began to wonder why? Amber didn't dwell on the fact that her boss was a vampire. But then, every once in a while, Amber fantasized that maybe she herself would get to live hundreds of years. And then she snapped back to reality. She needed to live this day, not some future century. And on this day, the FDA could come calling at any time.

She had trained the last group of staff the previous week. Amber stood at the front of the room, surveying their faces. "The FDA provides an important public service. They safeguard the health of the American people by making sure medical products like ours are safe and effective. And the law gives FDA great power to ensure that safety. If FDA became convinced our products were unsafe, they could prosecute anybody who works here—not just management. Their people can show up with guns and tell us to step away from the test equipment, make everyone leave the building and put a padlock on the door. Now, we know that wouldn't be in the best interests of our patients. So it's important that when FDA inspectors arrive—unannounced, as they always do—we answer their questions truthfully. And it's just as important that we only answer the questions they ask. Don't go overboard. Don't give a full recital of everything you do all day. And keep control of your records. Give the inspectors what they ask for and no more. Everybody clear about that?"

The staff nodded their agreement.

"Good. And keep in mind that we are due for an inspection. Like I said, we never know when it will happen. But chances are it will be soon. When you get back to your office, take a look at your records to make sure everything is entered correctly. Review your required training and check that you are up to date. Be sure to take the quiz from today's training so you get credit for being here. And remember: Just the facts, Ma'am, like they said in that old TV show. Answer the question and then stop talking.

"Alright. That is all."

CHAPTER FOUR

Luke Castleton parked in front of the home of his chief inspector, Rachel Sutter. The house was a single story, brick, with white shutters and a black front door with brass fittings. Trimmed bushes in brick planters, grass cut to a uniform three inches—everything neat and under control, much like Rachel herself, who emerged and locked the door. She was wearing her signature black suit. He had copied the look and they now appeared, he sometimes thought, like a pair of agents from *Men in Black* instead of the FDA.

As Rachel approached the car, Luke remembered fondly the first time he met her, when he was a new hire in the Chicago district office.

FDA had no funds for frills. Rachel sat behind the metal desk in her tiny office as Luke hovered at the edge of the only visitor's chair, afraid of making a bad impression.

Rachel spoke without preamble. "We are here for one reason only: to protect the public health. On my team, we inspect biologics. That means blood banks and companies that make blood-related products. I've been doing this work for thirty years and I have yet to encounter a blood bank with nothing to hide. They are very good at hiding, so we must be very good at finding. And we are."

He had nodded, impressed, intimidated. Unsure of what to say, he said nothing. She continued.

"You will find me a fair boss, a supportive boss, as long as you do your work. First, that means learning the territory. For the next two weeks you will do nothing but read. You will eat, breathe and sleep the biologics industry and FDA regulations. In the third week you will make your first inspection as my junior partner. Each time we inspect, you will gain more responsibility as I see that you are ready. People say I am a control freak. You may have heard that."

"No, I—"

"Well, they are right. To a point. I do like things to be in order. However, I also appreciate growth. Prove to me that you can do the job and I'm happy to share control of an inspection. Understood?"

"Yes, thank you, Dr. Sutter."

"Please call me Rachel. Save the formalities for when we inspect a blood bank. Materials are on your desk and loaded onto your computer. Now go read." She turned back to her computer. He was dismissed.

That was a year ago. And she had been true to her word, on all counts.

"Good morning, Chief." He glanced at her as he started the car. Rachel looked to be fifty something, attractive in that way women gain when their children have grown and they have time to take care of themselves. Office gossip was that Rachel and her now-deceased partner had two children a little older than Luke, both living and working overseas. Luke sometimes wondered if he was Rachel's office son. After that gruff talk in her office on his first day, Rachel had taken him under her wing and made sure he had everything he needed to succeed. Certainly more than he could say for his actual parents, who had pushed him out of the nest at eighteen with an audible sigh of relief.

"So tell me about the Lake County Blood Bank of Highland Park, Illinois." Rachel chuckled. "That name rolls off the tongue, doesn't it?"

These days she often relied on him to prep for their inspections.

"Minor infractions for late maintenance on test equipment. They corrected those within thirty days. No complaints filed against them, ever."

"I see. Either they are an especially good blood bank or they are a bad blood bank that's really good at hiding."

"My guess is they are a good blood bank. They've received very few citations over the last ten years. Only unusual thing is they have a night shift."

"Now that's interesting. I haven't run across many like that. This could be fun."

It was a warm spring day and for the rest of the trip they sat in companionable silence and listened to music—classical, Rachel's choice—and admired the scenery. Rachel wore sunglasses, as she was doing more often lately for headaches. The day before, she had spent the whole morning at a medical appointment. Luke wanted to ask how that went, but could not find the right words. None of his business, really.

It was an hour's drive from Rachel's home in Aurora to Highland House, their hotel, and just ten minutes more to their inspection site.

This week should be straightforward.

THE INSPECTION BEGINS

CHAPTER FIVE

The two agents presented their credentials at the front desk. Terry the receptionist knew the blood bank was due for inspection and—Ta-Da!—today was the day. She knew the arrival protocol by heart: Alert management, usher the inspectors to a closed conference room with no visibility to company operations, offer them coffee and donuts, and sit with them until management arrived.

First things first: Terry called the blood bank president. "Boss. They're here."

"FDA?"

"Yes."

"Thanks Terry. Please call Amber."

"Will do. We'll be in Conference Room A."

Marion thought back on all the inspections over the years: the earnest examination of records, the predictable questions and her staff's well-rehearsed answers. There was always some risk of exposing the true nature of the business, but Marion's experience had taught her that FDA inspectors were bureaucrats, pencil-pushers, devoid of the imagination and perseverance required to see the larger picture. They looked for trees and missed the great big forest right in front of them. This time had to be the same. Marion had confidence that she and Amber could deliver.

Beyond that, she was sure of two things: That what they were doing was the right thing, and that no one from FDA would ever understand.

~

The conference room was neat and clean, the table a polished black wood, the chairs maroon leather. On the walls were posters about the history of blood banking, from the early days to the present.

The inspectors sat with Terry and waited for management to arrive. After a few minutes, Rachel stood and perused the posters with interest. "Some of this happened a long time ago—even before I was born."

"I guess so, Chief, considering the first transfusion was in—what? —the sixteen hundreds?"

"Yes, Luke, very good. In England: A dog-to-dog transfusion; 1665, it says here."

Rachel continued her circuit. "And here's the first human transfusion: from a lamb to a man, 1667."

"Probably not the same blood type."

"Ha! No doubt. And here, from a cadaver to a young man, in Russia in 1930. They knew about blood types by then."

Luke shivered. "Grisly, all of it."

"But how else would we be where we are today? Oh—and here's the first ever blood bank, right here in Chicago. Founded 1937. Run by a woman: Dr. Elizabeth Schermer. Nice."

Marion walked in, with Amber close behind. "Thanks, Terry. Good morning, and welcome. I'm Marion Chase, blood bank president. And this is my VP of Quality, Dr. Amber Pettis. Greetings from everyone at the Lake County Blood Bank." Marion gave them her most practiced smile and took the measure of her adversaries.

The older of the two replied. "Hello, Dr. Chase. Rachel Sutter, senior inspector from the FDA district office in Chicago." Rachel stood ramrod straight as she shook hands with Marion and Amber. Her blond hair was cut in a pageboy, and her tortoiseshell glasses with trifocal lenses allowed her nearsighted eyes a clear view of her surroundings. Rachel was in her fifties, compact and self-contained. She gave off little in the way of pheromones or facial expression. Marion liked that: a mystery to solve. This should be interesting. And something else: Marion had another reaction which she pushed to the back of her mind.

Dr. Sutter continued: "And this is my colleague, Luke Castleton."

The young man with the bobbing Adams apple stood to shake hands with Marion. "Good to meet you." He was lanky, with a sweaty hand and a faint scent of anxiety. Marion was certain he was new, perhaps in his first year with the agency. As he greeted Amber and shook her hand, he had to hold his voice steady to keep it from quavering.

The four of them sat down and exchanged business cards. Rachel gestured at the box of pastries and said to Marion, "These donuts are quite good. Won't you have one?"

"No, thank you, I've eaten." Which was true. A nice AB positive, Marion's favorite, on the edge of expiry, straight from the fridge. Bracing.

Next came the standard ten minutes of chitchat before they got down to business. The weather. The drive from the district office. Yes, the hotel seemed adequate. Yes, they knew so-and-so who inspected two years ago. Yes, thank you, we are finished with coffee, let us help you clear the things.

Dr. Sutter presented the requisite papers, like the ones Marion had seen many times before, and gave the standard spiel. This was a periodic inspection, not the result of a complaint. The blood bank was required by law to show all documents on request. Inspectors would not examine financial records unless they became relevant. Records of acquisition, testing, and disposition of failed or expired blood were all in scope, along with the backgrounds and qualifications of everyone on staff.

"And so," said Rachel, "Let's begin with you, Dr. Chase. Tell us how you came to be head of this blood bank."

Marion was ready with the well-rehearsed pablum of a sanitized life. Just once she longed to tell the whole tale. Especially to this one, who called herself Rachel Sutter; this woman who evoked someone from her past whom Marion did not want to remember.

Marion was accustomed to the stream of faces, variations on a theme from one generation to the next. She could remain in the day, fixed on the task and the people at hand; beyond that, all humans blurred together. The mind can barely contain the memories of one lifetime, much less centuries.

At times a resemblance struck her. A face she passed on the street might conjure a medieval publican, long gone from the citadel at York. Or a store clerk's expression might bring to mind a soldier she nursed in the trenches of France in 1918. But the face of the senior inspector was more than an echo of another life. This was the true likeness of Cecily, the woman she adored in the village of Whixton, centuries ago; the lover Marion wished she could have saved. Her lover never lived to be the age of the woman who sat across from her now.

In dreams Marion allowed herself to remember Cecily's face. In her waking hours, in her professional life, she would never acknowledge the shock she felt when Rachel Sutter shook her hand.

Across the table, Amber wondered what was playing through her mentor's mind. Would they succeed in keeping the nature of their business hidden, once again? They were about to find out. Amber had coached the staff in every way for the inspection, with training, record reviews, even rehearsals on how to answer likely questions. Marion had been confident, cocky even; after all, no past inspection had come close to revealing their second business, hidden in a basement that was not on the floorplan.

They were ready for anything—except Dr. Rachel Sutter.

When they took a break, Amber pulled Marion aside.

"What's going on? Tell me."

"Later. I promise. Right now we have work to do."

When Rachel first laid eyes on Marion Chase, she could not help admiring the woman's chiseled features and salt-and-pepper hair. Rachel had started dying her hair blond when the gray came in early, and she saw no reason to stop now. She planned to stay blond until the day she died. But she did admire women, especially women leaders, who made a different choice. Dr. Chase wore no makeup and had sensible shoes—Rachel suppressed a smile at the old-time euphemism for Lesbians. *I wonder...* she thought, but then banished the question from her mind. If she had been alone she would have slapped her own hand for entertaining lascivious thoughts about the target of an inspection.

Dr. Chase launched into her prepared talk, projecting a floorplan onto a screen. "Before we tour the facility, Amber and I will give you an overview of our operation: How we acquire blood, how we test it, provide it to patients, dispose of tainted and unused blood."

Marion Chase projected a persona that was at once sympathetic and steely sharp. Her level tone, her measured pace, her command of FDA requirements, all gave the impression of a blood bank under full control. Her performance was clearly designed to reassure her audience that the organization ran like clockwork, totally dedicated to the safety of patients, ready and able to deliver the products they needed. This was a formidable woman in her prime. Chase appeared to be about fifty, which fit her *curriculum vitae*. There were a few laugh lines at the corners of her bright observant eyes; Rachel had the totally unprofessional impulse to reach out and touch those laugh lines, which she instantly quashed. In the back of her mind as she listened to Marion's polished introduction, Rachel wondered how long it had been since Marion touched someone; tried to remember for that matter how long it had been since Rachel herself was in the arms of another woman. She pulled herself together in time for the tour.

Just inside the double glass front doors, a clean lobby with two rows of chairs for waiting blood donors was backed by a large reception console. To the right of that room under a sign marked Donations, a door led to a clinic fully equipped to take whole blood, plasma, and platelets. Comfortable lounge chairs were flanked by all the needed equipment. Beyond that clinic was a recovery area where recent donors sat and sipped juice under the watchful eye of a nurse.

Behind reception was the testing area, taking most of the square footage of the building. Here blood was first typed and then tested for a variety of ailments, from HIV to hepatitis, Lyme disease, COVID-19, and other ills that could be transmitted by blood. The health of red cells was checked, along with other tests of viability. Rachel noted how blood bags were labeled, dated, and status marked as each test was completed.

On the other side of the reception area were the offices and conference rooms, the record storage area, and the changing room for staff. And of course there were rest rooms, storage rooms, and refrigerators filled with blood. Separate refrigerators housed blood just received, blood that had been tested, and blood ready for shipment to hospitals. Each unit was tagged with its stage in the process. And then, well segregated from useable blood, were the refrigerators for expired blood and infected blood. Each bag in those refrigerators was clearly marked for offsite destruction. Behind the testing area was an archive room where records were kept, and Shipping and Receiving, where everything that came in and everything that went out was identified and tracked.

Rachel's first impression was favorable. By all appearances, it was a smooth-running operation.

Marion's goal was to ensure that the hidden purpose of the blood bank stayed quietly in the dark. Any time an inspection happened, her mission was to project a transparency that maintained the illusion. And so as she led the inspectors on their tour, Marion considered how to contain each of her adversaries.

The younger agent, Luke Castleton, was the lesser challenge. He would likely spend his days in the archive room, poring over documents, lulled by the perfect record keeping that was a seamless combination of reality and illusion. Amber had created a few red herrings: small deviations that would give the junior inspector minor infractions to write up, so that he would feel he had done his job without repercussions for the blood bank.

The senior agent, Rachel Sutter, was another creature entirely. Sutter was a seasoned agent with a history of successful enforcement actions against the companies she inspected. Alert and stone-faced, she was the kind of agent who could see the big picture and not just the details. Well-tended records might not be enough to keep this one from realizing there was more to this operation than a standard blood bank. How to distract her? Marion thought about Rachel's demeanor during the well-rehearsed overview. When she met Rachel's gaze, their eyes had lingered just a moment longer than necessary. Marion saw something in Rachel that was more than professional interest. Perhaps desire was the key to keeping Dr. Sutter distracted. As they returned from the tour, Marion sent a brief smile her way and saw the roses rise in Rachel's cheeks.

Unless, of course, thought Marion, *that was my own wishful thinking.*

After the tour, Rachel asked Luke to begin inspecting the company records. Marion said, "Amber, could you show Mr. Castleton to the archive room?"

"Sure. Mr. Castleton, please follow me."

With pleasure, he thought but did not say. "Thank you," he mumbled, "Dr. Pettis." Shambling after her, he wanted to talk but had no idea what to say. She wore a solid maroon dress that was businesslike yet it drew his eye like a bee to a flower. Her earrings were gold and purple, and caught the light even in the dim hallway.

Amber opened the door with a badge that hung on a cord around her neck. "Here are the records for each batch of blood received from mobile collection vans in the last five years," she gestured. "All chronological. Over there are the paper records, and on these two computers are the scanned electronic versions. Just let me know what you would like to see, and I'll retrieve it for you and answer any questions."

"I don't want to put you to any trouble," said Luke. "I can find my way from here."

Not a chance, she thought. *There is no way I'm letting you loose in my archives.* "It's no trouble, really. I'm happy to help." Amber smiled. "You're my top priority today." She gestured for him to sit as she settled into a chair across from him.

Luke opened his notebook. "How about we start with the plasma records for the past six months?"

"Of course. Plasma is collected onsite, as you saw during the tour." She stood and pulled a folder from a file cabinet. "These are the paper records. And I imagine you'll want to compare them with the electronic versions, Mr. Castleton?"

Their eyes met over the conference room table. Hers looked friendly and open, while he cultivated a slight frown, his professional gaze, practiced at hotel room mirrors near various inspection sites for the past year. He doubted his frown fooled Amber for a moment. Her eyes were light blue, like ocean shallows on a summer day. He wanted to move closer to her, and maybe he would have were the table not in the way. Good thing it was there.

"Do you mind calling me Luke?" He blushed as he asked, which embarrassed him, and made him blush more.

She raised an eyebrow. "Are we allowed to use first names, Mr. Castleton, under FDA agent guidelines?"

He shrugged, tried to look nonchalant. "There's no one but us in the room right now."

"True." She smiled. "Alright then. For archive room purposes only, here are the electronic records, Luke. And please call me Amber."

He smiled back. "Thanks. Amber."

The afternoon passed pleasantly, with Luke reviewing what had to be the best-kept records he had seen at any blood bank in his short FDA tenure.

And then there was Amber. To Luke, she looked like an angel from a Renaissance painting, with her auburn hair and lovely round figure. Luke had never understood the attraction of thin women; they were too much like him, too angular to be attractive. No, give him the plump round body of a grown-up cherub to love. And the way Amber walked, that incredible sureness she had. Her confidence, too, was guaranteed to draw him like a magnet. *Get ahold of yourself*, he thought. *This woman works for an inspection target. That means she is off limits.* Until when, though? What about after the inspection? How long must he wait? Until all of their inspection issues were resolved? *Let's hope their issues are miniscule and few. And maybe I can offer her advice during the process?* Ugh. He was in trouble already, and they had barely begun the inspection.

Amber looked at her watch. "We're to gather in the main conference room at four," she said.

"Um?" Luke was intent on the stack of records before him. "Oh, right, that's coming right up. Say," he held out two pages. "In April you processed fifteen hundred units of blood. But you used close to two thousand labels."

"Oh. Right. Our printer acts up sometimes."

"Ah." He made a note, then stood. "OK, let's join the others."

Rachel had spent that afternoon poring over facilities drawings of water lines, electricity, and ventilation throughout the building.

"On our tour I counted eight ventilation systems with vents on the roof," she said. "But this schematic only shows four."

"Hmm. Interesting. I'm not sure about the difference," said Marion. "But Peter Short, our Facilities director, will be back from vacation tomorrow."

"Who is handling his job while he's away?"

"Our head custodian takes care of routine work. But he is not involved with system design." Marion smiled her most ingratiating smile. "That's the challenge with unscheduled inspections: we can't guarantee everyone is here. But I'm certain Peter will be able to explain it. I'll make sure he is available to meet you tomorrow."

When the inspectors were gone for the day, Marion and Amber sat down to debrief.

"Luke seems to be quite taken with me."

"That's useful. I love a good inspection seduction."

Amber smiled. "But on the other hand, when he isn't bumbling, he's pretty smart. He picked up on the extra labels we're using."

"Oh bother. What did you tell him?"

"I said our printer eats a lot of labels."

"That's partly true. Good one. But if they document it, we'll have to come up with a different way to disguise our label use before the next inspection. Plus we'll have to replace the printer."

"Oh, he's already written it up."

"Figures. Meanwhile our Dr. Sutter realized we have twice as many air outlets on the roof as we need for the main floor."

"Ouch. And Peter is back tomorrow. What should he tell her?"

"Maybe that it's a backup system? Or extras in case of expansion?" Marion shrugged. "I'll call Peter tonight and strategize."

Amber nodded. "These inspectors are too thorough for my taste."

"By the way, don't you know somebody who works at Highland House?"

"Yes. Want me to check how long their reservation is?"

"Please."

"And Marion...."

"Yes?"

"Have you met Rachel Sutter before?"

Marion looked away. "No."

"I saw the way you looked at her. What's going on?"

"She reminds me of someone, that's all."

"Someone from long ago?"

Marion nodded. "A very long time ago. When I was young, in Whixton."

CHAPTER SIX

From earliest memory, Marion preferred the company of girls. Boys were loud, bossy creatures, too full of themselves, while Marion's girl chums were beautiful creatures with long silken hair. When she reached her womanhood and the boys came calling, she was unmoved.

But she was moved by Cecily Dale, her dearest childhood friend. When Marion and Cecily were eleven, a healer named Bridget took the girls of the village on a pilgrimage to see Mother Shipton, the prophetess of Knaresborough. Shipton stood at the entrance to her cave, a lone spectral figure, this woman who prophesied the Great London Fire, to the amazement of Samuel Pepys and the royal court over a century hence. Mother Shipton signaled Marion and Cecily to step forward from the group of children. She took their hands and said, "Together, and apart, and then together again. Blood of your blood." Then she put their young hands together and smiled a kindly and toothless smile.

What did she mean? Marion wondered. And with her hand clasped with Cecily's, she noticed her friend's solemn beauty in a way she had not before. From that day Marion was smitten. Behind the church on a

Sunday when they were just sixteen Marion kissed Cecily on the cheek.

"You may do more than that, dear Marion," said Cecily, and she did. Marion kissed her Cecily full on the lips, and a sweeter moment she had never known.

Just then Cecily's sister Joan came round the corner and saw them.

"The devil will take you!" she cried. "Come to the priest at once and confess your sin!"

"What sin is it, to love your friend?" asked Cecily. But Joan was not moved. She towed the girls behind her to the church straightaway and in to see the new priest. He looked intimidating in his ornate robes, surrounded by Biblical paintings and stained glass inside the Norman chapel. But the priest was hard to convince.

"Young girls often show affection for one another," he said, and Marion silently blessed him.

"This was more than affection. This was the very sin of lust. I saw it in the eyes of that one—" said Joan, pointing to Marion.

The young women were sent to pray. From that day on, Cecily and Marion met secretly in the woods, with no one but birds and deer to witness their courting.

It was May and the grass was soft and green when they had their first tryst in a meadow outside Whixton. Cecily pulled Marion down beside her on the turf. Light purple bachelor's buttons and deep pink cuckoo flowers grew amidst the grasses. Cecily wove a flower crown for Marion's hair and said, "Now you are my lady fair, Princess Marion."

Marion blushed and shook her head. "I am none such. Let us be friends, dear Cecily, for you are no Lord and I cannot be your Lady."

"Just for today you can be Princess, my love. Pretend with me." Cecily leaned Marion back upon the soft grass and kissed her, kissed her with all the desire in her heart, with only the bees to see them, and no one there to interfere or judge. Marion knew her heart's delight in that moment. Cecily's breath mixed with her breath was sweeter than the scents of the flowers. When Marion stroked Cecily's cheek, her skin was smoother than a flower petal. They untied each other's lacings and slipped their dresses over their heads, then came together skin to skin, and their hands found each other's softest places. Even with their eyes closed, the light of the Spring day lit their way to one another.

Yet in her moment of bliss, Mother Shipton's words whispered in Marion's ear: "Together, then apart, then together again." Marion feared that the time apart from her love would come too soon.

After that day, when they saw one another in the village, Marion and Cecily acted friendly yet distant. They gave no one cause to suspect their trysts in the woods. But Cecily's sister Joan was not fooled. She persuaded their father to marry Cecily off quickly to John Draper, a widower ten years older.

The first time they called the banns in the village square, Marion shivered although it was summer. She had expected, this, but so soon? With Cecily betrothed, Joan kept a closer eye on her, and never again did Marion share the sweet grass meadow with her beloved.

Cecily was a stunning bride and not the first to be wed with tears in her eyes. Marion stood in the doorway of the church, unable to bear being there, and equally unable to look away from her love, who shone like a light from Heaven in her blue wedding gown. The bridegroom and everyone else in the church seemed to Marion to be mere shadows.

Once wed, John Draper set Cecily to work cleaning his house and tilling his fields, and caring for the children he had sired on his dead wife. From that day Cecily was lost to Marion. Their time apart in the prophecy had arrived, and Marion could not imagine how it would end.

To comfort herself, Marion took long walks in the forest. There she got to talking with old Bridget, the healer who lived in a cottage in the woods. When Marion first saw her, Bridget was out collecting herbs, brushing back her gray hair as she bent to pluck the green stalks.

Bridget knew without asking that Marion was brooding some loss, and she never pressed to know what it was. Instead, she began to teach Marion the uses of plants to heal. Rosehips to move the bowels, sage to move the bladder. Comfrey to bring on a cough when needed, yarrow to cure infection. Bridget taught Marion how to make a tincture, soaking the herbs for a moon cycle; and how to make tonics and poultices.

When Bridget's health failed, Marion cared for her until her passing. Marion stayed in the cottage, away from Joan and her wagging tongue, away from the sight of the lover she could not claim.

The old cottage was built of stone in the manner of the North, with a thatched roof. It had two windows, one at front and one at back, with sturdy wooden shutters that closed fast and locked from the inside. The door had iron latches and a thick wooden bar to set across. Marion lived there for years, safe in the sturdiness of the building and its strong door and solid windows. And until the last night she lived there, neither human nor beast ever gained access except by Marion's invitation.

At one side of the cottage was the garden, where she grew all the herbs that could be cultivated for tonics and poultices. The others, the wild herbs, Marion gathered in the woods near home. She loved to garden and was happy in solitude, though she enjoyed the company of those who sought her out for healing.

Inside the cottage was a strong oak table where she set her herbs for drying and grinding. Shelves held vials of remedies, all the way up to the ceiling, where she hid the most toxic mixtures on the topmost shelf. Mortars and pestles were her tools. Marion kept a pitcher of water filled from the stream for drinking and for creating remedies. In one corner of the cottage was a sleeping cot and underneath it her few bits of clothing. A small table in that same corner held foodstuffs, which she gathered in the woods or from the garden, or which grateful townsfolk brought when Marion's tonics helped them heal.

It was a safe place and a contemplative life, and she enjoyed it. The surrounding woods were green and glorious, and the ever-changing sky kept her company. Marion knew she was blessed to be there. She wanted for nothing, though she never forgot her Cecily. In that time and place, for a woman to have the kind of independence Marion enjoyed was rare and had its risks. To be a healer was to be an outcast, a woman at the edge of society. In the minds of many, there was at most a blurred line between herbal remedies and sorcery. Across Europe, independent women were being tried as witches and hung or burnt at the stake. And when King Henry VIII established the Church of England, anyone who did not accept the monarch's church became suspect.

And there was more. Sequestered as she was in the forests of Yorkshire, Marion nonetheless heard of King Henry's Witchcraft Act of 1541 that made it a crime punishable by death to practice enchantments. Molly, a woman from town, told Marion about the proclamation when she came to the cottage seeking a tincture for her child's cough. "And you know they are saying that herbal healing may be sorcery. But that's not what you do, is it, dear Marion? You are no witch. And we're all so grateful to you." Indeed, Marion believed it impossible that such troubles would ever arrive at her door. But then came a bright September morning, when she ventured into town on market day.

On that fine morning, Marion pushed a cart laden with her jams and jellies to the village center. She went to the village four times a year, to trade her preserves for the few supplies she needed: A pair of castoff shoes from the miller's wife, whose feet were very like hers; or perhaps a few candles. She never brought tonics or poultices to town; she waited for folks to come to her in private. Marion was early to market that day and found a good spot near the well, in the shade of an oak. Villagers began to arrive, singly and in groups of two or three, pushing their own carts and bringing coins—some of them debased with cheaper metals to fund the lavish lifestyle of their king. "'Tis best to barter these days," the man in the next stall commented to Marion.

She caught a glimpse of Cecily now and then on market days, always from a distance. But on this morning Cecily arrived with her stepchildren and walked right up to Marion. Without even a greeting she said, "I need a tonic from you. I must never conceive by my husband."

"Come to my cottage then. I have no such tinctures here."

"I dare not." Cecily hissed these words. Her eyes were wild, her hair askew. A young child twisted in her arms; the other two clung to her skirts.

At a stall on the other side of the well Marion saw Cecily's sister Joan, staring. "Your sister is watching."

"To hell with my sister. Do this for me." And she was gone, gripping the youngest, with the others trailing behind her and clutching her skirt as if holding a lady's train.

Before the day was out Marion had a message from the priest to see him on her way home. "Now, Mistress Marion, I have done what I can to protect you. I must warn you that your friendship with Mistress Cecily could bring you both to ruin. I have been patient but I must tell you that women have been pilloried for less. Do your penance now, and do not tarry with her again."

"I have done nothing wrong, Father. Cecily came to me seeking a tonic. There was nothing in this visit of love between women. I've naught to do penance for."

"Then you shall not receive absolution."

"Very well. I am resolved to stay completely away from Cecily. If she approaches me again as she did today, I shall run away. I can outpace her, burdened as she is with the brats of her husband's dead wife." And with that Marion returned to her cottage, pushing her cart before her. As solitary as her life had been, she resolved to avoid human kind even more.

Yet she was not completely cut off. It was not long afterwards that Marion received word the priest had been called to serve at York Minster, a great honor. The next priest was an even sterner man, more inclined to believe stories of witches and demons. And it was not long until Joan was bending his ear with tales of Marion having seduced Cecily.

One day in July Cecily appeared at the cottage door, out of breath, begging for a tonic to quiet her womb. She offered money which

Marion refused, and kisses which Marion likewise would not take. "You are married now," she said.

"To a man I despise," said Cecily. "Please. If you and I cannot be lovers, at least let me not die in childbirth with his brat."

Marion gave her what she asked for, a tincture in a small bottle, a concoction of herbs to prevent conception or even, in sufficient concentration, cause miscarriage.

Cecily uncorked the vial and smelled it. "Parsley? And pennyroyal?"

"Aye, and Queen Anne's lace, anise, and more. Just two drops, under your tongue, two weeks after your courses finish each time."

"I understand," said Cecily. "Thank you."

And she was gone.

～

Joan had no children of her own, and on certain days she came to the Draper house to help her sister with the stepchildren.

"I cannot wait until you have your own new baby," she said one day. "That husband of yours must be an eager lover. His first wife was with child every year—such a blessing."

"And look what it did for her, there in the churchyard under a stone. I need no babies; I have enough on my hands with hers." As she said these words, Cecily touched the handle of a tall cupboard but did not open it. She glanced at Joan and walked away.

Joan, curious, waited until her sister was out of sight and then opened the cupboard door. There, under a blanket, she found a small bottle. When she opened it and inhaled its aroma of parsley and pennyroyal, she knew why her sister was not with child a year after her marriage.

Joan hid the bottle back where she had found it and made her excuses to Cecily. She had to see the priest that very day. Joan had no doubt who had provided that wicked potion to her sister.

～

"Marion's lust knows no bounds. Until she is tried as a witch, she will keep interfering between man and wife."

The priest frowned. "And where is this potion you speak of? Have you brought it to me?"

"No, Father, I have not. But from its aroma I can tell you it contains a concentrate of herbs to prevent a woman from conceiving, and which a woman already with child must avoid."

"For what reason did you not fetch the vial for me to examine?"

"I am afraid of my sister's wrath, for she has given herself over to one who consorts with the devil."

"Your sister's failure to conceive in marriage may not be evidence enough. And yet, as a healer whose cures verge on sorcery, Mistress Marion is suspect."

"And there is the matter of her unnatural love for my sister."

"Which you alone have witnessed."

"It is said that Mother Shipton first put their hands together, and she is known to be a witch."

"That is true. Very well, I will write to the Assizes at York to find if they see fit to try Mistress Marion as a witch."

On a gray morning three months hence, a man arrived at Marion's door in a wagon pulled by a chestnut horse. Behind him in the wagon was an unfortunate woman from another village who was accused of witchcraft. The man tied Marion's wrists, lifted her and tossed her roughly into the wagon.

"Ye two witches can keep one another company," he said, "whilst I parade you through Whixton Village." He was as good as his word, taking his time coaxing the horse past jeering villagers, chief among them Joan, who looked on the passing wagon with glee.

Were I really a witch, thought Marion, glaring at her beloved's sister, *I would cast such a spell that you, Joan, would die on the spot.*

The wagon made its way down rutted pathways and late that

evening finally passed through the Roman walls at York. The city sits at a strategic location, on the ruins left by early Roman conquerors and later Viking invaders. Their wagon passed the Minster, the great cathedral, already centuries old, and arrived at the Assizes. Rough jailers led Marion to a cold moldy cell, where she must wait for the circuit judge to arrive. In one corner of the cell a pile of old straw was laid on the stained stone floor for a bed. With no receptacle for waste, past tenants of the cell had dedicated the opposite corner to their leavings. From the look of the stains, the long hems of the women's dresses had spread their waste across the floor.

Marion sat alone, the days marked only by one meal a day of moldy bread and thin porridge. To pass her days she called up images of her garden back home, now certainly wilting, and the inside of her cottage, where by this time mice had likely convened to nibble the herbs on the drying rack. Six weeks later, Marion was summoned to court, her dress hanging loose on her underfed frame and the hem stained with her waste.

The judge himself was bone and skin, as if he never ate a good meal. To calm herself as she stood in the dock, Marion imagined which herbs she would give this man who owned her fate, depending on whether she wanted him to gain muscle or waste away to nothing.

The judge consulted the warrant before him, a complaint from the priest at Whixton. "There are two charges in the case at hand. I see that this woman, Marion Chase, is accused of acts of lust with another woman. But I can tell you without reservation that relations between women are impossible. It is more likely for a goose to lay a Christmas pudding than for one woman to consort with another. Thus, on its face, this accusation has no merit. Now, as to the other charge: I see that Mistress Marion stands accused of witchcraft, in having given the subject of her supposed lust a tincture to prevent conception when that woman enjoys the marital company of her husband. This is a serious matter. However, we have received word that the woman concerned, a Mistress Cecily, has in fact conceived and expects a child of her husband. Therefore no charges have been proved. The case is dismissed."

Marion swayed in the dock. The tincture worked. She knew it. Once she heard of the charges, Cecily must have stopped using the tincture. As desperate as Cecily was to avoid pregnancy, she had sacrificed herself for Marion.

Before she ever reached home, Marion was plotting how to provide Cecily a tincture to end her pregnancy, a stronger version of the herbal potion used to prevent conception. But there was no way to reach her. Joan was furious at the judge's decision and roused the men of the town to a righteous fury.

And two nights after Marion returned to her cottage, the men of Whixton arrived, saving her from the wolf, but subjecting her to a different fate, and sealing Cecily's fate as well.

By now the sun had set, though in Marion's windowless office it was hard to tell. Amber had barely breathed through Marion's tale. "And Rachel Sutter reminds you of Cecily?"

"Rachel *is* Cecily, as near as I can tell, except that Cecily died so much younger."

"You're thinking of Mother Shipton's prophecy."

Marion met Amber's gaze. "I'm trying not to."

DEBRIEF, DAY ONE
CHAPTER SEVEN

At Highland House, Rachel and Luke unpacked in their respective rooms. Rachel found her quarters unremarkable, with generic art and the kind of furniture a person might assemble from a kit. But the bed was just right: comfortable and inviting, neither too hard nor too soft. She had a moment to lie down and think before she was due to meet Luke in the lounge.

Rachel Sutter was good at disguising what was on her mind. It came from a youth spent hiding science books from her mother, who believed in faith healing and was certain the earth was flat. Her mother had no idea how absurd all that seemed to her only child. As the daughter of a single mother, Rachel was careful of her mother's feelings. Her mother worked hard and was good to her. After she joined the FDA, Rachel began sending money home every month, and sometimes her mother even cashed the checks. She surely needed them.

So it was second nature to Rachel to remain impassive about her inspection findings, even while she gathered information. Some inspections were routine, with a few minor findings to report back to the agency. Some inspections yielded a pattern of neglect, where companies were lax in their duties and records were poor. But very rarely something else emerged: a pattern that pointed to a hidden secret, an organization that was deceptive or even criminal. Extra labels? Extra air vents? Meaningless, or clues to something bigger? It was too soon to tell.

But what Rachel did know, and was determined to hide, was her attraction to Marion Chase. The blood bank executive seemed to glow, had what skeptical Rachel refused to call an aura. Was it visible only to her?

Rachel remembered a moment that day, as they stood side by side looking at floorplans, when Marion was pointing out the blood testing process and brushed against her arm. It might have been accidental, Rachel thought. And it might not. Rachel hoped she was immune to such enticements. Yet she found herself replaying that moment in her mind: The stiff tweed of Marion's jacket against her wrist. The scent of Marion's perfume as she leaned in. The quiet sound of Marion's breathing next to her. If she were honest, Rachel had to admit that in that instant she wanted Marion to put an arm around her shoulder and say, "Let's ditch all this, shall we? Let's go out to lunch and have a massage and then nap in a big, comfortable bed in a really nice hotel— not where you're staying right now. I know just the place in Chicago: a spacious room, a bed with a canopy, and the best Italian dinners this side of Tuscany."

Oh the places your mind will go, thought Rachel. *Stop it. Stop it now. Get a grip.*

Was she, Rachel, becoming infatuated with the subject of an inspection? Should she step aside and call in another inspector?

No. She was an adult. She was rational. She could handle this.

Rachel went downstairs to the lounge and sat across a small round table from Luke. "What are your first impressions?"

He was still trying hard to impress her in that rookie way that reminded her of her son Victor, now so far away. Victor, who had grown from a thin and earnest teen into a confident professor. She was beginning to see that growth in Luke too.

Luke consulted his notes. "That label thing was odd. In an operation that seems so well-run, who would let a printer eat twenty-five percent of their stock?"

"Yes. It may be nothing, or it may be something. We'll dig deeper."

"But what could it mean?"

"Sometimes blood banks relabel units that are due to expire. They give them a later expiration date so they can sell them. I'm not saying that's happening here, but it's possible."

"And how would we find that? Examine their outgoing stock?"

"Exactly. Why don't you take a look tomorrow? And I will check their process for extending the date. It could be legit if they're retesting."

"Got it, Chief."

When she got back to her room, Rachel tried to get comfortable and scrunched the pillows on her bed. Usually she was asleep before her head hit the pillow, but on this night, with a full moon glowing through the curtains, sleep eluded her. She had more than the inspection on her mind.

For Rachel Sutter, illness was an inconvenience that seldom happened. It was something to set aside and rise above, an obstacle that she would not allow to interfere with getting the job done. She was, above all, a pragmatist. She thought little about tomorrow, thought little about anything, really, except what she was doing right now: Examining the paper trail of a blood bank and making sure they were keeping Americans safe. That meant they were doing the testing. Using the oldest in-date units first. Screening their donors. Maintaining their equipment. Rachel had been making inspections for thirty years, been through every epidemic or near-epidemic from HIV to Zika to COVID-19. She put her mind and heart into every inspection and if she'd believed in a soul she would have put that in too.

So it was with great reluctance that she had visited the doctor just before the inspection of the Lake County Blood Bank. She had found two lumps in her right breast: one in the breast itself, the other beneath her arm. She felt fine. She was sure it was nothing. But it was prudent to check it out. And so far, she had heard nothing. Best not to borrow trouble. With an effort, she put the whole thing out of her mind.

She could not help but envy women who could talk about such things with their mothers. But Rachel understood her mother's limitations. She knew her mother had grown up in a tumultuous time. She was patient with her mom. But Rachel was an independent thinker, the kind of woman who is anathema to a place like her home town.

~

As Rachel finally drifted into sleep, she remembered her last, rare visit to her mother, when she was surprised to find Jenny in front of a computer.

"Mom, when did you learn to use the internet?"

"Reverend Peterson led us in a class. We're tracing our ancestry as a way to mark our religious heritage."

Rachel took a seat next to her mom. "What is your goal?"

"I want to go back to the beginning of Protestantism. I believe our ancestors left the Church of Rome long before they came here to Zion." Her mother looked proud of their forebears.

Rachel looked at the screen, at the boxes and lines connecting people who died long before her mother was born. Her mother's mother's line, with its parade of different last names, led diagonally up to the right of the screen from the United States to England, where it finally came to rest at the very right corner with a woman born in Northern England in 1898. She was Rachel's great-grandmother. Her name was Grace Ann Hebroth.

Hebroth. What a funny name.

But when Rachel finally slept, it was not her ancestors but a certain salt-and-pepper blood bank director who haunted her dreams.

~

Early the next morning, Rachel asked Luke to extend their hotel stay. "We may be here awhile."

"Got it, Chief."

THE WOULD-BE ROCK STAR
CHAPTER EIGHT

Gregory Baines looked every bit the part of a rock guitar player. He was a small town success story, the kind of guitarist who puts on a better visual show than a musical one. With his dark hair swinging wildly as he played, Gregory was all black leather and thick silver zippers. Zippers were everywhere, on his leather jacket, his leather pants, his leather boots. His guitar was black with silver trim, specially decorated to match his outfits. He took himself seriously, his guitar playing not so much.

Somewhere along the line some groupie had been a vampire—fortunately for Gregory, a vampire with a thing for him. Although she was hungry, at the last second she switched from feeding on him and leaving him to die, to granting life eternal. Gregory was suitably grateful and kept her around for a few days, while he learned the tricks of the vampire trade and made sure his libido was not affected by his transition. No problem; if anything he was hornier than ever. It wasn't just sight and smell that was more acute for immortals; at times he suspected he had grown taste buds on his member. Gregory embraced his new lifestyle as a full-fledged vampire. He even turned the lack of sun to his advantage and made white makeup his signature look.

Amber and her friend Catherine met Gregory one night at a local rock-and-roll bar. They had a table near the stage for the ten o'clock show. Catherine managed to yell in Amber's ear between songs, "The guitarist is cute. In an eighties way. Maybe a little full of himself."

"You think?" Amber was amused by his antics, wiggling the neck of his guitar, bobbing his noggin and sending his full head of black hair flying. "He is a bit of a throwback."

By this time the guitarist had spotted Amber and seemed to be playing just for her, strutting rooster-like back and forth. Amber wondered whether female chickens found roosters' antics as amusing as she found his.

At the end of the first set, the guitarist took the mike. "Thanks everyone for coming out tonight. We're 'Dead Men Rising' and I'm Gregory Baines, lead singer and composer extraordinaire. Oh, and these are the other guys…" He introduced the rest of the band, then put his guitar in the rack and hopped down from the stage right in front of Amber and Catherine. He kissed each of their hands. "Ladies," he said. "How remarkable that we are all here at this very moment on this auspicious night. Enjoying the show?"

When the music was over and the instruments packed, Amber allowed herself to be persuaded to sit in the front seat of Gregory's car. As he kissed her, his teeth grazed her neck, and something about the sensation jarred her memory. "Have I seen you before? Maybe at the blood bank?"

Gregory sat up. "The blood bank? The Lake County Blood Bank? You work for Marion Chase?"

"Yes. I'm the Quality Assurance VP."

"Oh." He sat back, suddenly subdued.

"Why? Do you know Marion?"

"Yes. We go back. Way back."

"Ah! You're a vampire."

"Shh! We don't use the 'v' word around here."

"There's no one but us in this car."

"I know but—" he sighed. "I make my money by mimicking a vampire. I've got the hair, the big teeth, the pale skin. But nobody wants the real thing. The real me. They just want the pretend version."

Amber folded her arms. "You brought me out here to feed on me, didn't you?"

"What? Oh no. I would never. Well, maybe just a sip."

"And then you found out I work for Marion. And now you're sitting at the far side of the seat, not interested, because I'm not your dinner."

"Oh, Baby, trust me, I *am* interested. You are delicious. In every way, not just as a meal ticket."

Heaven help her, she did find him sexy, with his long hair and his fake bluster. She found out later that night just how sexy he could be. Who said that sex was just for the living?

What she thought would be a one-night stand turned into weeks and then months. In the midst of that rather torrid affair, along came Luke, whom Amber had orders to string along. That was easy at first; Amber arrived on that first inspection day with the frisson of lovemaking still lighting up her nerves like a neon bulb.

To Amber, Luke Castleton looked like one of those skinny boys she remembered from high school. His suit was just a little short at the wrists and ankles, as if he were still growing, even though he had to be pushing thirty. When he realized she was looking at him, he blushed beet red, and she gave him a bright reassuring smile. He fidgeted with his pencil then, staring intently at the table as if all the secrets of the blood bank were inscribed there. *This one will be easy,* she thought. *I can distract him from everything but me, with the tiniest encouragement.* The thought made her smile, just as if she were smiling at him.

"Men are so simple," Amber said to Marion after the inspection day ended. "I was just saying to this fellow Greg Baines last night—"

Marion looked up from her computer. "Sorry, whom did you say? Gregory Baines? Are you dating him?"

"Oh, we're not officially dating. We just get together. He's the singer for that local band, 'Dead Men Rising.'"

Marion hesitated. "Your social life is entirely up to you—"

"Why do I sense a 'but' here?"

"—And at the same time I'm happy to share what I know about Baines. Only if you want to know."

"Sounds like you have some reservations," said Amber.

"Mm."

Amber laughed. "You can't hint around like that and not tell me."

"Alright. We are here, as you know, in support of the ethical vampire community of Lake County. And to that end, we ask our evening customers to feed only on ethically sourced blood, from our blood bank or the blood of vermin."

"Yes, and...?"

"We have regular clients, some of whom you have met, who show up every few nights for supplies. And then there are the others: living dead who come by once a month or so. We provide them with blood, no questions asked, on the theory that we may be saving a mortal life every time we do. But there is no way to know whether their primary feeding source is vermin or human. We don't press them about it. Your friend Gregory is one of those who dips in and out of our services. Look at the database downstairs and you'll see."

"I won't spy on someone I'm involved with."

"No, of course not. Forgive me. But do be careful with him. Even if you are ready to become a vampire yourself—"

"Which I am not." Amber frowned.

"—and even if you were, you might end up as a food source, not a vampire, with that man. We have much more reliable friends who could help you transition if you wanted to."

"Thanks, but I don't want to. Maybe someday, and maybe not. I thought I'd have a one night stand with Gregory, if you really want to know, but it's evolved into something more like friends with benefits."

"I see. Frankly I don't find the male gender very appealing, but that's just me. Clearly you do find them attractive. Just be careful, is all I'm suggesting."

"Yes, Mother."

"I am not your mother. And if we were related, which I doubt, I'd be twenty generations back."

"Too literal."

Marion smiled. "I've been told that before."

INSPECTION DAY TWO

CHAPTER NINE

Amber and Luke returned to the Archive Room at the start of the second day so that he could look at records of previously transfused blood. Amber reached over to Luke midmorning to pass him a notebook and touched his hand, seemingly by accident. But the touch was quite intentional. She was conscious of her efforts to encourage him, to ramp up his level of interest, to ensure that whatever he might find in those pages, or for the rest of the day, would be overlooked or forgotten. Instead, it was Amber herself who was bewitched by that contact with this awkward man. She gave just the tiniest intake of breath when skin met skin. At that, he looked up from the records and smiled. "Are you alright? Do you need to take a break? We've been at this all morning."

She nodded. "Just need a minute," she said, and escaped from his hand and left the room. *Fresh air,* she thought. *Fresh air.* And out she sped into the sunshine, her chest heaving as if she had run a mile.

She blinked when she returned to the dim interior and found Luke hard at work, his head bent over the files as if nothing at all had happened. She took her seat and tried to put the whole thing from her mind.

Later when she passed her boss in the hallway, Marion whispered, "How's young Luke doing? Madly in love yet?"

Amber whispered back with a nervous laugh, "Oh, he's getting there."

~

Marion and Rachel spent much of that second day in the conference room, with Marion providing practiced answers to questions. Rachel's mind wandered as she listened to Marion. This was bad; Rachel's mind never wandered. She could focus on the most obscure details of equipment maintenance without ever losing the thread. But she found that when Marion spoke, all she could think about was what it would be like to walk up to the woman in the middle of her next sentence and take her in her arms.

They were in the same conference room as on the first day, surrounded by posters about the history of blood banking. Absurdly, Rachel noticed a resemblance between Marion Chase and an early transfusion doctor. Except he had a mustache, and must be long dead. *Pull yourself together*, Rachel thought, and managed to speak with authority.

"We've noticed you are sending blood for destruction at the four-week mark."

"Yes," said Marion, meeting her gaze.

"FDA guidance says you can ship blood taken as long as six weeks ago."

"True. But as you know, Dr. Sutter, there is no bright line between good blood and bad. Red cells deteriorate gradually over time. Once they are bottled, they begin to change shape and don't fit through capillaries as well."

Rachel nodded. "I'm aware that studies show cardiac patients who receive blood near the expiry have a lower survival rate."

"And yet it's permissible to provide that lower quality of product."

"The problem, of course, is supply. Dr. Chase, how does your blood bank succeed at obtaining enough blood to meet demand while sending only newer units?"

Marion smiled. "We are especially good at outreach to the community. Amber Pettis does a lot of that work. We've established a terrific partnership with our town."

"You must have; you supply blood to hospitals as far away as downtown Chicago."

"Indeed."

"Alright." Rachel tapped her pencil on her notepad. "Understood. Next, I'd like to inspect the outside of the building, and the roof."

"I'm sure Amber can assist you with that."

"Why not you, if you don't mind my asking?"

"I sunburn easily."

"You're a brunette. Dr. Pettis is a redhead."

Marion smiled. "Go figure."

Rachel caught up with Amber on a break. "Come up to the roof with me for a few minutes, if you don't mind."

"Of course." *What now?*

Rachel carried the building plans with her up the stairs and gestured to them as she and Amber stood on top of the building. "You have vents here and here on the outside of your building that don't show on these plans," she said.

"Really?" Amber could feign ignorance when it suited.

"Really. When did you say your facilities director is available?"

"Peter Short is just back from vacation this morning. Let's pull him into a meeting with you and Marion."

"Yes. Alright. And by the way, I've asked Luke to take a look at your process for destroying expired units. Could you assist him with that, after we're finished here?"

Destruction of old blood was a vulnerable point; Amber considered the options. Their records looked pristine, all managed by the trusty night staff. All the old units appeared to be shipped out and their destruction validated. But if the inspectors went so far as to check on the units actually received at the destruction facility, everything would start to unravel. But first things first: The meeting with the head of Facilities.

Peter Short had no idea why there were extra vents on the outside of the blood bank, and he did not want to know. What Marion Chase did in her unofficial basement was none of his business. All he knew was he despised government regulators. Whatever they were after, they were not getting it from him.

Rachel spread out the floorplan on the conference room table and Peter gave it a glance. "Thank you for pointing out this omission. We'll be sure to add these vents to our schematic and submit to you."

"And about these vents—what is their purpose?" Rachel would not be put off so easily.

Peter dismissed them with a wave of his hand. "They're nonfunctional. At some point there may have been plans to add another floor. That was before my time. We keep the vents as a backup in case of future expansion." Pretty flimsy, but the best excuse he and Marion had come up with on the phone last night.

"Thank you." Rachel was skeptical, but what else could she ask, for now? "Can we expect the revised schematic by the end of the week?"

"Sure. And if there is nothing else?"

"Much appreciated, Mr. Short. I understand that this first day back from vacation is a busy time."

That night, Luke and Rachel huddled at a café down the road. Rachel set down her coffee cup. "Every time I think I understand what they are doing, I'm wrong. They are not relabeling to extend expiration dates; if anything they pull them in. And yet, something is going on here. Maybe like nothing we've seen on any other inspection."

"You mean, something wrong, maybe criminal."

"Maybe so. I'd like to believe Marion—Dr. Chase—is not capable of that."

"And why do you want to believe she's not?"

Rachel crossed her arms. "Because I—I don't know. I just don't want to believe they are doing something monstrous."

"They? Or her?"

"What?"

"Nothing. Never mind." Luke looked away.

Rachel frowned. "Luke, if you have something to say, please say it."

"It's not my place. You're my Chief, not the other way around."

"I want to hear what's on your mind. Spit it out, Luke."

He squirmed in his chair. "Dr. Sutter—Rachel—You don't have to be the agent who uncovers whatever is going on here. We can back you up. Bring in another inspection lead from Chicago."

Rachel shifted uneasily. "And why would you want me to do that?"

"I don't *want* you to, exactly. But I've seen the way you and Dr. Chase act when you're together. And I wonder if your feelings for her interfere with conducting this inspection."

"Luke, that's an insulting suggestion."

"I'm sorry. I would not bring it up unless I was confident that something is going on with you and this blood bank president. Emotions that could interfere with the conduct of the review. Believe me, I have no interest in your personal affairs."

Rachel nodded. "Alright, Luke. Let's turn the tables here. I've noticed the way you look at Amber Pettis."

Luke shook his head and looked down.

"Don't deny it! You are head over heels for that girl."

Luke dug the toe of his shoe into the rug like an embarrassed kid on a ballfield. "Do you want my resignation?"

"No, definitely not. Let's just both of us set our feelings aside and do our jobs. I'll keep Marion at arm's length and you do the same with Amber. Can you do that?"

"Yes." He looked her in the eye. "Can you?"

"Yes. I certainly can. Alright then. Carry on."

~

Marion and Amber debriefed in Marion's office.

"I suppose you could kill her," said Amber.

"Yes. How delicious. A nice O negative."

"How do you know that?"

"A girl senses these things."

"A *girl?* Really? How old are you?"

"Five hundred and twenty. But you know, seriously, when I came up in the Sisterhood at York, we were taught to protect women. Only kill in self-defense, and even then kill only men. This business with Rachel doesn't meet either criterion. So no fresh blood for me."

"Then how are you going to stop her?

"I don't know. But I do know that if she disappeared, the next inspector they sent would be even more suspicious. And I can't kill the whole FDA district office."

"Much as you might enjoy it."

"Yes, actually, in my worst moments that does sound appealing."

"Is this one of your worst moments?"

"Not sure yet. Let's see if we can wiggle our way out of this."

"Alright. But first, tell me about this York Sisterhood of yours."

Marion smiled. "It was not as benign as it sounds."

THE CITY OF YORK, 1544

CHAPTER TEN

As their horse carried Marion and Vivienne toward York, a cloud passed in front of the moon. When the moon emerged again, its light seemed so bright that it blinded Marion for a moment. She turned to Vivienne behind her on the saddle. "What's happened to me? Why is the night so bright? And why am I so strong? I should be dead."

"Perhaps I should have left you for those fools to burn. Perhaps you are the greater fool."

"Tell me what happened. How did you change me?"

Vivienne coaxed the horse to a tree near a stream, dismounted, and gestured for Marion to sit with her on a fallen log. "Listen to me," she said. "The life you had is over. It's not just that those fools burned your cottage and destroyed your life's work. You'll have plenty of lifetimes to make that right. It's also that you have a different life now, with new strengths and new weaknesses. You need never fear man nor beast again. They cannot hurt you, not with knife nor fang. No one can hang you nor burn you. No jail can contain you. Mortal disease cannot touch you. And you will outlive every enemy you encounter. But heed this: you are vulnerable to the sun. You must hide from its light at all costs."

"What? Surely there is a potion for that."

"There is not. Should you create one, there are those who would pay handsomely. And also, you can never taste food nor drink again. You will be sustained by the blood of mortals or beasts."

Marion made a face.

"Do not turn away in disgust. This is your life now. Live it with honor."

"What honor can there be in such a life?"

"You will live in service to others. You would have done so, even if you had not killed yourself. But now you'll live differently than I expected."

"How so?"

"I had thought to bring you to the Sisters at the Convent, women whose skills as healers are unmatched, and who live in the blessing of the church."

"Take me there. I am tired of being persecuted for my gifts."

"I cannot. When I brought you back to life, you came into a life that is outside the church. There is a place for you in York, though. You will live on Grape Lane in the Sisterhood at Camden House, which is a brothel."

"A brothel! I cannot live in such a place."

"Do you believe you are too good for that? Too pure? And what other choices do you know, for a nocturnal woman? Indeed, I too wish for more choices between saint and sinner."

Marion thought of nothing to say, and kept silent.

They remounted, rode on, and passed through the gates of the Roman Wall, whence Marion had left after her acquittal, and thence to Grape Lane, the street of prostitutes. The Sisters lived in a two-story building with timbered walls and an overhanging second story, within sight of the great cathedral of York Minster. When they arrived at Camden House in the middle of the night, Marion was surprised to see that the lights were on and the front door was ajar. From inside came the sounds of drunken men and laughing women.

Vivienne explained their destination as they approached. "The women here keep each other company and watch after the mortal women who sell their bodies on the pavements of Grape Lane. In this house, on this street renowned for its brothels, the vampire Sisters are known as ladies of the night—which of course they are. The house is managed by a man they tolerate, and it amuses the women to dally with the men of the town. So, you see, you'll be in good company."

Marion was not so sure. "But why do women accused of witchcraft bed with men?"

"Shh. Don't let them hear you ask that."

"It's men who wanted to hurt these women."

"No chance of that, not anymore. One of these women could break ten of these men at a time."

"But why entertain them?"

Vivienne shrugged. "They seem to enjoy it, somewhat. It is not the life I would choose."

"And what do you choose?"

"I defend women where I can, from all manner of evil, such as almost befell you."

As they dismounted, Marion said, "Lying with men does not appeal to me. Can I come with you instead?"

Vivienne looked at her. "I'll stay on a few days, to see you are settled. And perhaps someday you can join me, when you are ready. You're a bit unseasoned for the work I do. Stay here a few years and then talk with me again. Now come and meet Sarah, who will tell you the ways of this place."

Sarah met them at the door and took them to a quiet room, away from the throng in the main hall. "Those who live in this house take a vow: Although we are destined to feed only on blood, we do so with the full knowledge that our continued lives depend on the deaths of others. Therefore we pledge to feast only on vermin: the rats in the gutters and those men who choose to hurt others. We will never hurt the innocent. We will never hurt children. We will protect the women of the street by feeding on the men who injure them."

Sarah pulled aside a window curtain. "We in this house are safe. But look out there, see the women of the street? Unprotected, they wait to be intimate with strangers. They know no other way to live.

And we who are strong can protect them." Sarah shut the curtains in anticipation of the rising sun.

Marion frowned. "But you too give your bodies to men."

"We do. Consider how few ways there are for women to live in this world. We are not like our sisters in the convent; we are weaker than they because we cannot survive the daylight. We are stronger than they because no man can harm us. In concert with those convent sisters we are formidable."

Marion mulled over what Sarah had said. "And I must ask: Do you enjoy this life, this closeness with the physical bodies of men?"

"In our mortal lives we Sisters loved the men who were good to us, and we loved their bodies. We still enjoy men's touch, more than ever now that we have nothing to fear from any man. And what of you, our newest Sister Marion? How have you fared with the touch of men?"

"I have never lain with a man. I have only lain with another woman."

"So you do not know whether it would bring you joy?"

"I do not know. But living here, I suspect I will find out."

"And are you willing to take our vows: To foreswear taking the blood of living humans, unless one human harms another? And to protect the women of this city?"

"I am willing, and I will abide by your code. I will try the blood of vermin and protect the women of York from harm."

"Then merry meet, Sister Marion. With you we now have our full complement of twelve Sisters. Let me show you to your room."

After seeing her small, windowless room, Marion went back downstairs. The women were gathered in the massive kitchen with men in attendance, most half drunk, while the women drank nothing. In the corner a man played a lute while a woman sang.

Marion found a seat in the great kitchen with the others. She was troubled that living here she must allow men to touch her. Having almost been burned alive by a crowd of men, the thought did not sit easily. A man who was tall and wide, almost a giant by the standards of the day, pulled up a stool and sat with her. Marion told herself she had nothing to fear. A man? Maybe it would not be so bad.

"Gentle lady, I see that you are new here. I am Albert the bawd of this house. Before I allow my customers to taste your wares, I will try them myself."

And before she knew it, Marion was led by the hand up the stairs to her small cell of a room, and Albert was pulling at his breeches.

In private his expression was different, impatient. "Take your own clothes off, woman. You cannot expect me to give such courtesy to one such as you." He pushed her toward the bed.

She wondered that the women of this place tolerated him. "And what would I be, then?"

"A common stain, you would be." He slapped her then, not hard, but hard enough.

Marion's strength was new, but she was beginning to understand her power. She put one hand around Albert's throat and lifted him into the air, his member swinging crazily. "I am no stain. I have never lain with a man, and by all that is holy, you will not be the first."

His expression changed from astonished to amused and he laughed, despite the tight grip on his throat.

"The virgin whore," he wheezed, and laughed again.

Marion closed her grip and held on as he twisted in her grasp. At last he was still. Then Marion did as her body told her: she put her lips to his hairy neck and drank, until she drained his body dry. Then she threw Albert's body onto the bed and left the room, taking her candle with her and closing the door behind her.

She walked down the hall. "Sarah!"

"Yes. Wait, he's almost finished."

Marion stood outside Sarah's room, disgusted by the view through the open door. Sarah lay all naked, her legs spread, while a clergyman still wearing his robes pushed into her. With one final thrust he grunted and collapsed on the bed, oblivious as Sarah left his embrace.

They stood in the dim hallway, Marion fully dressed and Sarah naked. Marion led Sarah to her room and told her what had transpired.

Seeing Albert's corpse, Sarah swore a great oath, retrieved her clothes and threw them on. "If anyone asks, he is drunk and we are taking him to his carriage and sending him home."

"And what will we really do with him?"

"You'll see."

Sarah and Marion trundled the body of the bully downstairs and piled it roughly into a cart. The body was lighter than it looked because it was drained of blood. His blood cells lit up Marion's insides like glow-worms, each one a pulsing source of life after life. She was horrified and delighted. "I drained him dry."

"Your first human kill," said Sarah. "You're going to feel so strong you could deal with his corpse yourself. But this time I'll come with you."

They covered the body and pushed it out the door, then turned right into Langton Lane, a twisted covered corridor with walls so narrow they almost touched the sides of the cart. At the end of the lane, they crossed a cobbled street and turned left into another tight passageway. This one led to the Sisters of the Convent.

Sarah knocked on the door, and a nun, seeing Sarah and the cart they brought, opened the door wide. Inside they were met by a kitchen nun sweating in her robes, making the morning bread for the poor of the city. In the warm kitchen other women in nun's habits cooked something in huge pots. Sarah followed Marion's gaze. "All these mortal women are accused witches saved by Vivienne and others of the vampire Sisterhood."

The kitchen nun gestured to them, "In here." In a darker room two women sorted clothes and jewelry. Without a word they began to remove the clothes from the corpse.

"What are they doing?" Marion asked the nun who had received them.

"The clothes will be washed and then given to the poor. The body —I'm assuming it's been bled—"

At this, Sarah nodded.

"—the body will be butchered and cooked into soup, again for the poor."

Marion stared at the nun, all dressed in the sacred robes of her calling. "I was sure that nothing more in this place could surprise me. And yet I am amazed."

As luck would have it, when they made their way back to Camden House, two other women began to load another body into the empty cart. One of them, a wiry woman named Sybil, turned to Sarah. "This one boasted that he had killed a woman on the street."

"Aye," said the other woman, Kate, as she covered the man's body with a blanket. "And then he tried to kill Sybil."

"You did well," said Sarah. "The poor will be generously fed today. Sister Marion killed Albert when he turned on her."

"Well done," said Kate. "The man had outlived his usefulness."

Sarah turned to Marion. "With Albert dead, we must find another man to be our procurer. The men of York will never accept a Madam."

Marion uncovered the dead man and began to strip the clothes off his body.

"What are you doing?" asked Sybil. "At the convent they donate these clothes to the poor."

Marion pulled on the dead man's doublet and boots. "You won't need a man for a bawd if I wear these clothes."

"You want to be the brothel keeper of Camden House?"

"I do. And I certainly don't want another such as Albert touching me." Marion finished putting on the dead man's clothes. "I never much fancied the idea of lying with men."

"Too bad you became a vampire, then. The convent sisters are left pretty much to themselves." Sarah lowered her voice. "I've long suspected the priest who leads them might have breasts under his cassock."

Marion smiled. "I'd like to meet this priest."

Dressed as a man, Marion could walk the streets of York at night unmolested. She would pass the women of the street and nod to them, speak with them courteously, and ignore their requests to purchase their services. But on a night that one of the women was attacked and beaten by a customer, Marion took that man down a dark alley and drank his blood until he was dry. The woman remained slumped on the ground.

"Sister, can you rise?" Marion gently helped her stand.

"Yes, I am alright."

"What is your name?"

"Anna. Anna Marshall."

"Here, Mistress Anna, let me walk you home."

"Thank you, Sir. But I cannot go home without coins in my pocket, or my husband will beat me. I will stay on this corner and look for a gentler customer."

"Your husband puts you out onto the street?"

"Yes. Many of them so treat their wives, the ones having trouble earning money themselves."

"What do you charge?"

"Depends on what you wants, Sir. But I could not charge you. Not after you saved me."

"Here." Marion put money into her hand. "Now may I see you safely home?"

"Oh, Sir, that is far too much."

"Save some for tomorrow night so that you need not endanger yourself. I'll walk by and see that no one harms you."

Marion made her rounds after that, twice an evening, alternating with watching over the women at Camden House. She convinced Sarah to spell her, and take up men's clothing when Marion walked abroad.

It was Sarah's first time in men's garb, and as was traditional for vampires, Camden House had no mirrors.

"How do I look, Marion?" Sarah smoothed the breeches and tunic that had lately graced a violent man and were now hers. "Am I convincing, as a man?"

Marion laughed. "You'll convince them well enough, even if you must settle them down from their brutish ways. No man can match your strength, Sarah, even though you're a bit on the slight side."

"Another night, when you are here, Bawd Marion, may I walk the streets of the town as you do, as a man among men? I would like to see how different it is to be treated that way."

"Of course you may. It's good practice, for we know not what the future holds." Indeed there was much uncertainty. The leaders of York were ambivalent in their support of King Henry VIII, risking the king's ire. And Henry was capable of much. When his nephew James, the king of Scotland, refused to convert from Catholicism to Henry's new Church of England, Henry's army attacked Scotland with a brutality that seemed destined to level the country or beat it into submission. That war was still ongoing.

But for now, there was enough trouble in Grape Lane to keep the women busy. One night when she came by Anna's corner, Marion found her on the ground, again bloodied and unconscious. Marion picked her up and carried her to Camden House. Sarah opened the front door and said, "Bring her to the small parlor. Sybil, fetch the doctor." Sarah turned to the other Sisters and their customers looking on from the parlor. "Now the rest of you, stop your gawking."

Kate organized a song for the clientele while Marion lay Anna gently on the parlor couch. She held the wounded woman's hand and could feel her pulse slowing, becoming irregular. Sybil came back quickly with the doctor, but he shook his head. "Not even bloodletting could help this unfortunate."

In her guise as a man, Marion shook the doctor's hand and thanked him warmly. What he had said about bloodletting gave her an idea. She turned back to Anna and overheard Sybil, as she walked the doctor to the door, asking, "Sir, could you say more about bloodletting?"

"'Tis an ancient form of healing," Marion heard him reply, as their voices trailed into the distance, "passed down to us from Hippocrates...."

No one had explained to Marion what to do, but a powerful urge to save this woman overcame her. She closed the parlor door and put her teeth to Anna's throat. She nuzzled at her neck, not sure how to begin. But once her teeth pierced skin and artery she felt a sureness she had never felt before. It was marvelous, it was ecstatic. She took in every drop of the woman's blood, so amazingly good, so totally different from the bits of red liquid she ingested each night from the rats in the lane.

As Marion drank, Anna's newly dead body quivered as if still alive, until Marion had consumed every last liquid morsel. And then, as if she had done this a hundred times, Marion knew exactly how to bring Anna back to new life: Marion pushed up her own sleeve, ripped a tear in a vessel at her wrist, and held her arm to Anna's dead lips. At once those lips quivered and suddenly Anna's jaws fastened on Marion's wrist, compelling the blood in Marion's arteries to flow into Anna's thirsty mouth. There was nothing dead about her now. Anna was like a howling babe, sucking for sustenance. Every tissue in Marion's body was starving for blood. Such pain, everywhere, all at once.

And at the same time pictures flashed before Marion's eyes: scenes from Anna's life, the proud wedding day, the craven husband who put her outside each night and locked the door until Anna came home with enough money from selling her body that he would let her back in. The encounters with customers, some indifferent, some cruel, the occasional one who was kind. They saw her not as a woman, not as a person, but instead as a vessel for their manhood. And, indeed, she was not a woman, not any longer; she was now something less and something more. Much more.

When Anna awoke she looked confused, and then, as she moved her hands across her skin and looked down at her new self, she grew angry.

"What am I now? A creature forever damned?"

She lashed out then, with a strength that surprised Marion. It was a scene Marion was becoming inured to: the sight of an immortal woman taking on a man. Only in this case the "man" was Marion herself, an immortal dressed as a man. Marion defended herself but struck no blows, waiting for Anna to tire herself.

But Anna was far from tired. She struck Marion again, with a force that would have felled any mortal. "Am I no longer a woman that I can strike such a blow?" Anna paused and regarded Marion more closely, where their struggles had pushed aside Marion's cloak so that the contours of her breasts pressed against her tunic. "But what is this? I see that you too are woman, and of the same stuff as I am now. I will not waste this new strength on you; indeed, I will not waste my blows on any woman but will go forth and destroy those who have hurt me. I shall begin with the one who set me on this cursed path."

"Who would that be?" Marion remembered the flashing pictures of Anna's life, even as the question formed in her mouth.

"My lawful wedded husband, who forced me into the life of a trollop. And whatever else I am, trollop I am no more."

With that she slammed from the room and then out to the street, closing the door behind her with such force that the door veered from its hinges.

I would not want to be that man, thought Marion. *Not for all the ships at sea.*

"**S**ister, we do not create more of our kind without permission."

Marion returned to Camden House shortly before dawn to find Sarah waiting for her.

"We did not mention it in our vows because we did not anticipate it would happen for you so soon. But it is our way. If every sister created as many of our kind as she pleased, we would be hard pressed to find our dinner. And we might turn to draining the innocent, contrary to our vows. We are surprised you could accomplish this thing without instruction; yet it does show that this life suits you."

"This life does indeed suit me. And the feeling of creating another of us is powerful."

"Yes, it is. And did you instruct this creature properly on her strengths and limitations?"

"I did not. There was no time. She left precipitously."

"You had not inquired whether she actually preferred to live again as one of us?"

"No, I had not."

"Marion, I understand you were granting her a boon; and yet you have loosed an untrained terror on the town. We shall see what comes of this. But you may need to intercede."

"I understand."

"And in future you will conduct yourself accordingly."

"I will."

There was gossip afoot the next night about the death of William Marshall, who had been the husband of the streetwalker Anna. And where Anna had gone no one seemed to know. The night after that, the pub was awash with talk of the death of George Grosvenor, another who had frequented the late night alleyways. And they said that Grosvenor, like Marshall, had been found drained of blood. By the night after, when Mark Smyth was found dead and bloodless, the streets had emptied of men and only women dared be outside by moonlight. "We are safe but we'll be hungry soon," one prostitute remarked to Marion, surprised to see someone she thought was a man abroad in the night.

There had been no time to explain to Anna the rules and limits of her new life, and so it was no surprise when the flurry of bloodless corpses ended. Marion searched the town by night until she came upon a pile of ashes outside a shop—ashes entwined with the wispy remnants of Anna's yellow gown. The prostitute vampire had taken her revenge, briefly, and been lost to the sun.

I will carry on her quest, thought Marion. *We will rid this town of a different form of vermin.*

Over the next two years Marion accumulated an entire male wardrobe, piece by piece from the corpses of miscreant men. She continued going out on nights when Sarah stood in as bawd, stopping violence against the women of the street. Once she paused under a street light and a woman touched her arm. "Where did you get that hat?"

"In a stall at the Shambles." Not true, but it must do.

"That hat belonged to my husband who disappeared."

"I am sorry." Marion took off the cap and offered it to the woman.

"No, I want nothing that belonged to that bastard. I hope he is dead. I take in washing now, and my life is hard, but so much better for his absence."

Marion was glad of her Sisters' faith in allowing her, a newcomer, to be their figurehead in the community. Over time, Marion came to know her eleven Sisters. One of them, the soft-spoken Gwen, told her stories of Sisters past. As they stood in the halls of Camden House, Gwen whispered of their Sister Delia, who could no longer bear the sunless sky of night and had stood, arms outstretched, awaiting the dawn. When dusk came, Gwen gathered her friend's ashes and put them in a jar on the parlor mantle, where her Sisters could keep her company. Marion came to learn that death, real death, unawakened death, was something the Sisters did not dread. They could survive knife wounds, take down a wolf, were unfazed by disease, and did not know senescence. They were notably fearless. But this one thing—sunlight—reawakened their fears.

Marion came to love the night. She loved the stars, which in those days were brilliant against the dim city lights. For Marion, as for all of her kind, night vision was spectacular. When she saw the trees at night, they glowed with a dark purple and their leaves susurrated. The eyes of the owls and the deer struck sparks. It is a special kind of magic, the vision of a vampire by night. And yet Marion missed the day terribly and wanted that freedom back—but not enough to sacrifice her new life.

~

A public house called The Green Man was around the corner from Grape Lane, on a narrow market street called the Shambles. Dressed as a man and going by the name Martin, Marion visited the loud and busy pub once or twice a week to hear tales of happenings near and far. Laughter and chatter echoed from the beamed ceiling as men sat at long plank tables trading stories. Marion listened more than spoke, nursing a pint of ale and slopping a bit onto the floor now and then to disguise the fact that she could not drink. One night she stood near a fellow from Manchester as he told of King Henry's new ban on bawdy houses.

"He says they are a scourge on a Christian nation. Can you imagine? And how does he know? Which stews does *he* frequent? They must be pretty bad!"

The fellow next to him said, "I heard they closed down the ones in Southwark, where the French Disease is everywhere. All the trollops were arrested. Bet the sheriff got it without paying for it that night!"

"Aye," said the man from Manchester. "Here, I have it: the King's Proclamation says no more *'toleration of such dissolute and miserable persons as have been suffered to dwell in common open places called the stews without punishment or correction for their abominable and detestable sin.'* Gather ye rosebuds, gentlemen!"

They raised their glasses.

"In fact," another man said, confidentially, "I hear the King's men are heading for York next. Unless you brought your money with you, it may be too late! And you, Martin—" This addressed to Marion. "—you may have claimed freedom from disease one too many times."

"Aye," said a man across from them. "And even if men do not leave your house with the French Disease, some have ventured into your establishment and never been seen again. When the King's men arrive, they may well visit Camden House first."

The conversation broke up into general murmurings, under cover of which Marion put down her mug of ale and made her way back to Grape Lane.

After Marion learned that the king was closing the bawdy houses, she gathered the Sisters together in the downstairs parlor. "King Henry is determined to close every brothel in England, and the word has it that his men are headed for York."

There were voices of concern, over which Marion said, "Sisters, we are well positioned to use this news to our advantage. Unlike others in the trade, we have a number of choices."

Kate scoffed. "Yes, all of which involve daylight. What does that leave us? I say we wait them out."

Marion ignored that and continued. "We are strong, but we are not invincible. All that the King's men need do is come into our home at midday when we are fast asleep, open the shutters, and we are ashes, every one of us. No, I say we don men's clothing, take our savings, and go our separate ways. Think on what skills you have that you could use at night. Once you pass as men, you could become night watchmen, or work in hospitals by night. You could run pubs or even run bawdy houses in other countries. I hope someday the Sisterhood can reconvene, but for now, we must part company."

There were murmurs of agreement.

Sybil called out, "We could become actors, if we dressed as men— and then dressed as women again."

That one got a laugh.

Marion continued, "Indeed. While our options as women are narrow, we expand our choices if we dress as men."

Lillian said, "And where would we get enough men's clothes for all of us?"

Marion pulled at her tunic. "I've saved outfits from men who attacked us and who are no more. I'm glad to pass some of this garb to my Sisters. Anyone else kept souvenirs?"

"Aye," said Sarah, and several others.

"Alright. Let's share with one another. Everyone back here in half an hour."

Marion guarded the front door, turning away clients gruffly, saying the wenches were all engaged for the night. When her Sisters returned, Marion gave them the location of a cave outside York where they could find refuge in the morning. They dispersed by twos and threes, leaving by the front door as if they had been late guests to their own brothel. Gone were their long skirts and cinched waists, replaced by the tunics and breeches of deceased male clients. The Sisters stumbled as if drunk, when really they were adjusting to the feel of men's boots on their feet. It was a moonlit night, and they wore their men's hats low to conceal their faces.

The cave where the Sisters gathered was near an ancient stone circle called the Twelve Apostles. The women slept all the next day and then gathered at the stones for their final goodbyes, hugging and exchanging plans.

Marion stood with Sarah at the edge of the circle. "This place is oddly named. Methinks these stones were here long before the Apostles were born."

Sarah laughed, running her hand over the rough edge of a standing stone. "You could be held for heresy, Sister, were you not already despised as a witch and a trollop."

Marion smiled. "I wish you well, Sarah. May you be safe and happy. And woe to all rodents wherever we go."

The women gathered in a circle at the center of the stones and named their intentions.

"I'm off to be a barber surgeon," said Sybil. "Why waste all that blood from bloodletting?"

"A grand plan, Sybil. May I join you?" asked Lillian.

"Aye," said Sybil. "We'll open a shop together."

"I'll be a trollop again, this time in Paris," said Kate.

"And I am happy being a bawd, which I learned thanks to Marion," said Sarah. "So, Kate, perhaps we'll find places in the same brothel."

Each woman in turn named her destination. Gwen would be a rector and help families bury their dead. "And relieve the poor bodies of their blood, while I'm at it." Flo and Eleanor would try their hand at acting. "'Twill be rodent blood for us, then," laughed Flo. Paulina and Alice would be nurses, caring for the sick at night in a London hospital. Bea and Theda were off to be nighttime explorers, dressed as men. "We'll find a good place to settle somewhere on our adventures," said Bea.

The Sisters put their hands together at the center of the ring and chanted, "Merry meet, and merry part, and merry meet again." It was a clear night, and the moon rose between the ancient rocks. Off went the Sisters, in all directions from the twelve stones. The Sisterhood was no more.

Vivienne arrived in York the following night, dressed in men's attire. Intent on saving the Sisters from King Henry's men, she hurried to the door of Camden House, and found the place dark and locked. A few unhappy customers pounded on the door and called out to no avail. Vivienne broke down the door and walked through the empty rooms with disgruntled customers trailing behind her. There was little to see but discarded skirts and corsets.

"Who was their bawd?" Vivienne asked one of the disconsolate men who traipsed through the cold rooms.

"A fellow named Martin," he said, and described the man to her.

Marion, she thought. *The wench has become a man.*

On her way out of Yorkshire, Marion stopped at Whixton, hoping to see her lover Cecily. She went to John Draper's house at twilight and found the door ajar. Inside a woman rocked a young child in her arms, in a chair facing the fireplace.

"Cecily!" Marion reached out, ready to embrace her. The woman turned. It was not Marion's love. It was her sister Joan, with a girl child in her arms.

"Where is she?"

Joan looked Marion up and down. "And there you are, dressed as a man at last."

"Where is Cecily?"

"You'll find her in the graveyard. She died bringing this one into the world. She asked us to name the child Marion. Of course we did no such thing. This is Baby Grace, the only reminder we have of the woman you brought to ruin."

Marion reached out to touch the child. Joan stood. "You shall not touch her. Get thee gone!"

Just then the widower came home from the fields. "What is this then, Joan? Why have you not made our visitor welcome?" He looked at Marion. "Oh. It is you. I should kill you, here and now, for your sinful lust after my wife."

Marion put one hand around his neck and lifted him from the ground. "Your threats are empty, John Draper. I could end you easily enough, and this horrible woman too, and I would, in spite of my vows, except that would leave the child without family. Take good care of young Grace, for if she does not thrive, I will be back for both of you." She dropped him to the ground then and went to visit Cecily in the village churchyard. There Marion shed the saltless tears of a vampire and cursed Mother Shipton for her empty prophecy.

"What's that you said? 'Together again?' What manner of togetherness is this, for me to stand at her grave?"

Marion travelled to France, where she heard of the queen's difficulties producing an heir and offered her services as a healer. Her success at helping Catherine de' Medici become pregnant and deliver a son made Marion a fixture at court. She found the men of France easier to abide, and because of her favored status, less likely to call for her execution as a witch. Eventually Marion became the mistress of a Count and Countess, and refined her skills at lovemaking with the pair. The palace cellar held plenty of rats to keep her fed.

It was not of course as good as human blood. Nothing could be. But Marion would not be a vampire who hunted for human blood. She was a healer, not a killer.

When the Count and Countess died childless, their fortune came to Marion.

. . .

Vivienne had been right: The Enlightenment came, finally, and people no longer persecuted witches, because the idea of witches was simply not logical. Back in England, the Witchcraft Act of 1735 made it illegal to accuse another person of supernatural powers. And supernatural powers included vampires, another illogical myth. Who could prove that anyone or anything lived after death?

When Marion's tale ended, Amber was silent for more than a moment, absorbing what she had heard. She imagined her boss sucking blood from rats, and tried to merge that image with the cool professional she knew Marion to be.

"So, you're rich," she managed, finally.

Marion laughed shortly. "Yes. But all the money in the bank could not buy me one meal in a restaurant."

"And that's why we're here? To be a restaurant for you?"

"Maybe more like a grocery store than a restaurant."

"You bleed us for food the way farmers milk cows."

"That's not quite fair. We help mortals too. But I understand; this must be a lot to take in."

"It is," said Amber, "even for a former Goth like me."

Marion stared. "You were one of those? A young girl painted up like a comic book vampire?"

"Now it's my turn to shock you," said Amber, laughing. "And about time, too. Yes, I was one of those. Should have put it in my resume, as it turns out."

Marion smiled. "I've sometimes asked myself how much truth one mortal can accept."

"And tonight I wondered that myself," said Amber.

THE INSPECTION, CONTINUED

CHAPTER ELEVEN

It was not just the cat-and-mouse game that intrigued Marion, although she was captivated that this Rachel, this FDA inspector, was so keen, so skilled, so eager to pierce the veil and learn the secrets of the blood bank. Marion had always been able to distract inspectors with a professional sounding line, with a well-placed smile just bordering on flirtatious. The fact that Rachel seemed immune to her wiles was maddening, a bit frightening, and alluring too.

Sometimes when they spoke, their eyes met, and unlike anyone she had known over the centuries, she could see nothing in Rachel's eyes—no emotion, no unconscious enlarging of the pupils. How could this woman control not just her expression but even her reflexes? And yet Marion suspected that much was happening in the mind behind those eyes.

While passing documents, they brushed hands by accident and Marion was shocked to feel a wave of emotion.

So that's where she hides her feelings, in her touch.

But was it Rachel's emotions she was feeling? Or did Marion sense her own feelings when she touched this woman? Perhaps Rachel's pheromones were just as opaque as her expression. Perhaps Marion herself was falling in love.

No, not good. I can't afford to feel anything but wariness here. I must stay on my toes.

As Rachel grew closer to exposing everything about the blood bank, Marion grew closer to falling in love. When she slept she dreamt that Rachel was in her arms, and that her guarded gaze had gone, replaced by the steady open-eyed wonder of a lover in heat—a gaze she had seen only once before, in the woods near Whixton long ago. In her tiny cell of a bedroom under the blood bank, Marion tossed in her sleep, gripped by impossible passion. It was seldom wise to love a mortal, and disastrous to love a mortal enemy.

Marion could not know that at the hotel, Rachel dreamt of her too. In Rachel's dreams, Marion was an overpowering lover and Rachel, who was always self-contained, even in lovemaking, lost her control and submerged in passion like a swimmer pulled under by a great current. Yet she was not afraid. Just the contrary: In dreams, Rachel reveled in her abandon.

Professional that she was, Amber set aside her feelings about Marion's latest round of revelations and showed up for the next day of the inspection. That morning, Amber was retrieving records from a high shelf, standing on a step stool, and Luke, standing next to her, was very aware of her legs beneath her short skirt. To distract himself, he climbed up on a chair. Towering over her, he reached for the box of records, stepped down, and put them on the table. When he turned back to Amber, she was climbing gingerly down from the chair. Without thinking, he gave her a hand and, as her face passed his, kissed her lightly on the cheek. "What?" she said, turning her face up to his. "What are you doing?"

"Sorry." He blushed, let go of her hand and opened the records box. "Listen, I'm fine here, if you want to go."

"No, I'm assigned here, I'm not supposed to leave."

"Well, I'm glad of that. I promise to behave." *For now at least,* he thought. He glanced up and caught her smiling to herself. *Does she think her charms will distract me from my job? Or did she enjoy my touch?* He wondered which it was. Right now he did not trust himself with Amber. He had to get out of the archive room to somewhere more public.

"How about we switch gears and visit Shipping and Receiving? Dr. Sutter asked me to review your disposal process."

"Alright," said Amber, "I'll lead the way."

Standing at the dock with Burt Geisler, the shipping manager, Luke asked to see the outgoing records for the past thirty days. Burt opened a computer screen and showed Luke the folder as Amber looked on.

"These are hyperlinks to the documents for each box shipped from the dock. Here...." Burt stepped aside and let Luke take the computer mouse.

Bad move. Amber wanted to chime in, but restrained herself. She had trained Burt and his staff, and Burt knew to show FDA only and exactly what they asked for. He should never give control of his computer to an agent.

"Thanks." Luke clicked on the list of incoming shipments and opened several items while Amber fumed. Then he accidentally hit the tab for incoming materials, and after that, out of curiosity, opened a link to incoming supplies.

"How often do you order blood bags?"

"That's a standing order, once a month."

"Why so many? You're ordering a third again as many bags as the blood bank ships in a month."

Burt opened his mouth but no words came out.

Amber could not let this go on. "That question is outside Burt's purview. We'll need to check separately about blood bag wastage."

"Uh-huh." Luke had moved on. "And, sorry, but why order red food coloring? And what's this order for cornstarch?"

Burt didn't even open his mouth for that one.

"Oh," Amber jumped in and forced a laugh. "That was just silly. It was for a Halloween party."

"But why a *gallon* of red food color? And *ten pounds* of cornstarch? That must have been some party."

Amber shrugged. "You know blood bank people. When we do Halloween, it's all about fake blood."

Fake blood. That got Luke thinking. What if they were making fake blood, putting some kind of mixture into those extra blood bags and labeling them with those extra labels—that hadn't really been chewed up by the printer? They could be sending fake blood to be destroyed. What they sent could be catsup, for all anybody at the disposal site cared. They were destroying something that looked like blood and getting paid for it. But that begged the question: What were Amber and Marion doing with all their expired blood?

"**D**amnation," Marion said later when Amber described the scene that morning in Shipping. "After all we've been through, to think that bags and labels could bring us down."

"Like Al Capone going to prison for tax evasion."

"Thanks. I really appreciate being compared to a notorious gangster."

"Sorry, Boss. Maybe the saving grace will be Rachel's crush. I see the way she looks at you in our briefings."

"She may be taking a bit of a shine to me. Don't know how much good it will do."

"Uh-huh. And I see the way you look at her too."

Marion's eyes widened. "Me? Absolutely not. I am acting. I am, after all, a practiced seducer. Half a millennium will do that. Did I take you in when I gazed at her with longing? I'd like to think I took her in too."

Amber shook her head. "You were more convincing when you talked about drinking her blood."

That night at dinner, Luke and Rachel brainstormed over big portions of mediocre food at a nearby diner. Luke toyed with his fork. "What do you bet they're selling almost-expired blood to places with big shortages."

"You mean other blood banks?"

"Probably."

"But why just whole blood?"

"Maybe it's not just whole blood. Maybe plasma too—that's easier to fake."

"True. We know about the whole blood because of the red food color."

"And the cornstarch."

"Yes, the cornstarch. But they need a place to make this stuff. And bag it."

"They must have a whole separate operation. But where?" Luke looked out the window at the scene in the well-lit parking lot, and the blood drained from his face.

"What's wrong?"

"Oh. Nothing. It's just Amber, kissing some long-haired guy."

Rachel looked out the window. Amber was clearly having a good time. "I'm sorry, Luke. But this really proves that she's been leading you on—in the same way that Marion is leading me on. It could be a deliberate distraction. A strategy. A way to take our attention away from the fact that they are hiding something."

Luke was still staring at Amber. "Yes. I didn't want to believe it. I thought she liked me. But there it is."

Marion and Amber sat waiting for the inspectors.

"Amber."

"Yes."

"I smell something on your skin. Have you been seeing someone?"

"Well… yes. I didn't know it was that obvious."

"It is to me. Smells like that renegade vampire, Gregory. I thought you'd dropped him."

"Wow, that's…"

"What?"

"The fact that you can smell *him*, specifically, makes me think about all I'm missing as a mortal."

Marion raised an eyebrow. "True. Like having to worry about getting toasted to a crisp by a ray of sunlight."

"Yes, that's fair."

"Or having to move every decade and leave everyone you know behind, so they won't figure out that you never age."

"Alright, I see what you mean."

"Or sensory overload because your brain isn't set up to smell every single molecule that drifts your way. Or burying your friends, the way other people bury their beagles."

"OK. I get it. Being a vampire isn't all gin and bananas. But would you rather have died in the fifteen hundreds?"

"No. Becoming like this was better than being burned as a witch. It was also better than committing suicide to avoid being burned as a witch. But it's not something I would willingly choose at your age and give up my mortal lifespan."

"You have a point."

"Not to mention you seem really friendly with Luke. Or is that still about getting him to see things our way?"

Amber sighed. "That is what's so crazy. Greg and Luke both appeal to me, in different ways."

After all, Gregory had beautiful skin. It was chalk white and contrasted almost shockingly with his hair—hair so black it had a blue sheen, like a blackbird's wing. He was tall and lean and muscular. He must have been an athlete and retained that build as a vampire, thought Amber, when she was thinking at all, which was not often while in Gregory's presence. He seemed to live for sex. It was the kind of sex you read about in stories; the kind where there is no room in your mind for anything except that moment, that passion, the way he gripped her skin in his hands, the way he inhaled her scent, kissed her neck so hard it left bruises.

She asked him once if making love with a mortal left him wanting a different kind of satisfaction and he chuckled. "You hit the nail on the head. It's like you're holding out on me, even though you're not. You are a wonderful lover. I just always want more," he said, nibbling her neck, her favorite place. She shivered just thinking about it.

Gregory brought up making Amber immortal again and again.

"But I'm enjoying the life I have right now," she would tell him.

"Think how much more you would enjoy it," he would say, "if you knew it could last forever."

She always changed the subject, but knew he would come back to it. She tried to think just of the present. In this moment, she loved his touch. She loved going to hear him jam, watching him play guitar, seeing his effect on the crowd; the women especially. She loved knowing that he was going home with her, not with any of them. His long dark hair waved as he played, his muscular form gyrated on stage. Only she knew the feel of that dark hair in her hands. Only she felt the trace of the callouses on his fingers from hours on the guitar, that rough touch on her thighs that let her know lovemaking was near. The anticipation was almost the best part.

Almost. Not quite.

The best part was feeling his body inside her, so strong, so cool. Kissing him and feeling his legs entwined with hers.

Late one night in bed, he had said, "Look at you, at the peak of your beauty. I want to keep you like this forever."

"Don't you think older women are attractive?"

"Hmm?"

"Like Marion. She's beautiful."

"Ah, Marion. That woman is a force of nature. But she isn't

scrumptious. Not like you. Just think: Your beautiful fleshiness could last for all eternity."

"Sometimes I think you'd rather eat me than make love with me."

"I don't want to eat all of you. Just take your blood. And give you mine, of course. Make you an immortal."

"How do I know you wouldn't just eat and run?"

At that, he threw his head back and almost howled. "You don't know, my sweet." He twirled one of her red curls around his fingers. "You just have to trust me."

Trust you to preserve me like a bug in sap, at the exact stage of a woman's life that you find most attractive? She almost said it aloud.

Amber considered what else she would give up if she acquiesced. Children? She shivered at the thought of half-vampire children. Was there such a thing? And did she want to experience every part of life, or keep re-living this one? Did she want to be cute and spunky forever? Or become an eminence, a presence, like Marion?

Now that Luke was in her life, she needed to decide.

Later that day when Amber smiled at Luke, he frowned, remembering her parking lot kisses with another man. "I know you don't really like me. This flirting is about the inspection, isn't it? This is about giving me just enough encouragement that I won't write up your blood bank. Believe it or not, this has happened to me before. I've only been with FDA for a year and somebody else already tried it. The first time I almost believed it. Not this time."

Amber shook her head. "Luke, I won't deny that's what I was doing at first. I was using my looks to get what I want. But that's changed. I've gotten to know you and I like what I see."

"Do you like me enough to tell me what's really going on at this blood bank? Because I keep thinking I understand it and then I keep finding out I'm wrong. Something is different here. And I don't know what, not yet. But I will find out. And if you're breaking half as many laws as I think you are, I won't be able to keep you out of jail. And I wouldn't, even if I could."

~

Gregory's band was leaving at midnight for a series of gigs across the Midwest. "It's no Rolling Stones tour," he said, "but we're pretty jazzed."

"Have fun," she said. "I'll miss you."

"Will you? I wonder."

After they made love he looked at her appraisingly. "Darling Amber." Gregory massaged her shoulders, traced one finger against the curve of her cheek. "You are luscious. Just the way you are, right now. Look at those breasts, that smooth skin, those lovely legs." He kissed her. "These juicy lips. Let me help you stay this way. You know how it works: Give me your blood, I give you my blood, and voila! You're immortal. Unchanging. Young and lovely forever."

"But what if I want to keep changing?"

"And why would you want to do that?"

"What if I want to be a mother? A grandmother?"

He shrugged. "There are plenty of people in the world. Why make more?"

"Even if I don't decide on children, what if I want to see what my face looks like as it matures? What if I want to become softer, wiser, the way my grandmother was wise? She was beautiful. She had such nobility, she had elegance. There are things you can't get by staying young."

"I cannot believe you keep turning me down. Look around you, look at movies and magazines and the internet. It's all about youth. Who could walk away from all that? Given a choice, who could let it slip through their fingers?"

Enough. Amber stood, picked up her clothes and began dressing. "I could, and I am. Watch me."

"A million girls would kill to get what I'm offering."

"Great. Go find one."

"I could force you, you know. Unlike your blessed Saint Marion, I don't always ask for consent."

She pulled on her jacket. "But you won't force me. Marion told me you come to them for blood when you need it. I've seen the units in your fridge, all lined up to take with you on tour. The blood bank people would cut you off in a second if you hurt me. And they would do more than that. They'd stake you out just before dawn where the sun would find you, and leave a bottle of sunblock just out of reach. Imagine how pretty your skin would look when the sun hit you."

"Alright, don't get your panties in a knot. I'm not going to make you do anything. I just can't believe you are passing up a chance to—hey, where are you going?"

"Where I should have gone already. To try and put things right with Luke."

"Your mortal goody-goody? Alright, if that's what you want. A houseful of snotty babies, then wrinkles? And Alzheimer's? Great. When you could have had the world, Baby. The world. But you go for it." He raised his voice at the end so she could hear him, but Amber was already gone.

When Marion touched Rachel's hand in the conference room the next day, she told herself that she was keeping up a faux flirtation to distract the FDA inspector from her job.

That's certainly how Rachel took it. "I'd appreciate it if you would stop this façade, Dr. Chase. Whatever you think you are doing, your efforts to be friendly are misplaced. I have my duty and I will execute it."

"So sorry—don't know what you mean—didn't mean to offend," Marion mumbled. She could barely maintain her demeanor at the sudden craving that overcame her when she touched the other woman. It was not the longing for a lover's touch. It was not the memory of her long-lost Cecily. Instead it was a blind hunger to feed, to devour, to suck every drop in Rachel's body and give nothing in return. What was happening? How could she, who had upheld her vows for five hundred years, be consumed with blood lust for a woman? And not just any woman; this woman, who was so like her long-lost Cecily?

Filled with shame, Marion stood. "Excuse me, please." She fled the room. This craving was impossible. There was no excuse. She had no explanation.

A CALL FOR RACHEL
CHAPTER TWELVE

Marion recovered herself sufficiently to bring a stack of company records back to the conference room. But as she approached the doorway, she heard Rachel's phone buzz and stopped just outside the door.

"Yes? Dr. Miller?"

The call was not on speaker, but with her heightened hearing Marion could make out a few words from the physician on the phone: *Malignant... Metastasis... Liver... Possible neurological involvement...*

"Oh. I see." Rachel kept her voice steady. "Can you say more about treatment?"

Next Tuesday... Surgery then radiation... Possibly chemo depending on...

"Alright. Understood. I'll clear my calendar. And prognosis?"

Wait and see. Best to get affairs in order. Sorry not to have better...

"My affairs are always in order, Doctor. Right. See you Tuesday, then."

Marion backed up so that she could stride into the room as if she had not heard, but she could not keep the look of concern from her face. She heard herself saying, as if someone else were talking, "Here are the records you requested." She set the stack of folders on the table. "But it's almost five o'clock. Maybe you'd like to hold off until tomorrow?"

Rachel laughed, a short sharp laugh. "Not sure anything can wait for tomorrow." She looked at Marion. "You know, don't you? How much did you hear?"

"Too much. More than I wish I knew." Without thinking, Marion sat down and grasped Rachel's hands in hers. "I'm so sorry, Rachel. Let me know how I can help."

As much in shock as Rachel was, she felt a frisson of joy at Marion's touch. And just as suddenly she was filled with a sadness so profound that it bent her body forward; grief for the life she would never live, with this woman or with any lover.

Marion patted her back, murmuring soft reassurances as if her adversary were a frightened child.

Rachel sat up and shook her off, wiped away tears, straightened her shoulders. "I cannot give in to this," she said, not knowing whether she meant this terrible diagnosis or the completely inappropriate attraction she felt to the head of a company she was inspecting—a company about which she had serious misgivings. She wanted to ask, flat out, *What are you doing here? What are you hiding? Just tell me. There is no time to hide.*

But no. She had to find out for herself. She had to come back from this fascinating and dangerous woman with evidence—evidence she could give to FDA, regardless of her own health. It dawned on her that this might be the last assignment she would ever work on. At that thought she almost shed tears but then was gripped with a steely determination to see it through. Next Tuesday? That was four days away. She could find out a lot in four days.

Marion watched a parade of expressions cross Rachel's face: Hard and determined, yet frightened. A flicker of affection, and then Rachel narrowed her eyes and controlled her expression. The fact that Rachel could take such command of her own emotions left Marion feeling even more protective of this woman who still had the power to destroy every dream she cherished.

Marion pulled away from Rachel just as the conference room door opened to admit Luke and Amber. They could hardly miss the emotion in the room, even though both Marion and Rachel tried to look as though nothing had happened. Would Rachel tell Luke? As if on cue, Rachel looked at Marion and shook her head, *no*. Marion nodded; it was not her news to tell. Although Rachel was seriously ill, until she saw fit to call the inspection off, it would continue.

But in that moment Marion understood the blood lust that had overtaken her. Like a lion stalking the weakest in a herd, Marion's predatory instincts were aroused by Rachel's progressing illness. Now, thank the Goddess, compassion prevailed. Through her sadness Marion felt just a hint of relief.

Rachel was determined to press on. "Let's continue for another hour. But first, let's take a break, shall we?" A few minutes later she came out of a stall in the ladies' room to find Marion near the sinks. They came together and Marion traced one finger down the side of Rachel's face, then lifted Rachel's hand and kissed her fingertips, one by one. She took Rachel's hand, led her into a stall, and closed the door. There she lightly touched Rachel's arms, her shoulders, her back. Then she leaned forward for the gentlest kiss and whispered in Rachel's ear. "I've never kissed an FDA agent before."

"This is kind of a first for me too."

The bathroom door burst open and two lab techs took stalls on either side of theirs, talking and laughing. Marion put her fingers to her lips, and then to Rachel's lips. She opened the bathroom stall and they crept out, as near to silent as they could manage.

"That was a close call," said Marion when they left the bathroom.

"Too close, Dr. Chase," said Rachel, and her tone let Marion know it would not go well for her if she mentioned the last ten minutes to anyone. Anyone at all.

~

The best way to stop obsessing about her illness was to keep alert and keep working. Rachel rounded a corner in the blood bank hallway and saw a lab tech in a white coat walk into the supply closet. She realized that Marion, next to her, was walking just a bit more quickly than usual, speaking more rapidly than usual, as if to distract her. But from what?

"We are looking at a pathogen inactivation process for blood as an additional safeguard, on top of standard testing for infectious diseases. What are your thoughts about those methods?"

Rachel nodded as if listening closely. As they approached the door of the closet, Marion's gestures became broader, as if to draw Rachel's attention. Marion was to her right and the closet door to her left. Without a word, Rachel opened the door of the closet and turned on the light.

"Ah! You can see how we organize our supplies, with those purchased first at the front of each shelf..."

"Someone walked in here and did not come out."

"What? I'm sure there must be a mistake."

"Is there a back door to this closet?"

"You've seen the floorplans, Dr. Sutter. There is no back door here."

You just kissed me and now I'm Dr. Sutter. Rachel was too busy looking for the latch to say it out loud.

When she felt the button on the back of the next to top shelf, she pressed it without saying a word. The back of the closet swung away and revealed a flight of stairs leading to a basement that was not on the floorplan.

Which explained the extra air vents. But what about the extra labels, and the extra blood bags, and that crazy order for red food color and cornstarch? Nothing to do with Halloween, certainly. Rachel was sure the answers were down these stairs.

Still silent, Rachel walked down the steps, ignoring Marion's voice behind her. At the bottom of the stairs were refrigerator cases with bags of what appeared to be whole blood. And there were other cases of what looked like blood but not under refrigeration.

And in the middle of the room was a lab, where two lab techs in white coats worked in silence. The workers turned to look at Rachel but turned back without comment.

Rachel faced Marion, her hands on her hips. "This is not blood bank equipment. This is a research lab. Or a small-scale formulation lab. Tell me you're not making street drugs down here."

Marion shook her head. "We are not making street drugs. We are making—or trying to make—artificial blood. Have been trying for some time now. Without great success, so far."

"Alright. I'll assume for the moment that you're telling the truth. In which case this is a research lab and outside the scope of my inspection. But why hide it? Why down here in the basement?" She looked around for the answer. "This lab is only half the size of the upstairs. What else is down here?" Rachel waited. Marion did not speak. "Well? You have a lot of explaining to do. Now, Dr. Chase, why don't you tell me what is really happening here. To whom are you selling old and contaminated blood?"

Marion shook her head. "It's not what you think." She opened the door to a small conference room just off the lab. "Please step in here, where we can speak quietly."

They sat at a small table. Marion closed the door.

"First off, Rachel, I want to apologize for not being completely transparent with you."

Despite years of training, and in spite of her worries about her health, Rachel had a tough time not laughing at that one. "I know the game. I ask questions, you tell us the minimum. Yes or no, if possible. Why would you give more thorough answers to anything?"

"Because you are too smart to accept made-up stories." Marion hesitated. "They say that truth is stranger than fiction and in this case it's very true. Because the truth is—" She took a deep breath. "—I'm a vampire. I helped develop blood banking, a hundred years ago. And I'm committed to providing ethically sourced blood for Midwestern vampires who choose that way of life."

Of everything she could have said, Marion had chosen the one thing Rachel never expected to hear: An admission of madness from a blood bank director. *At least,* thought Rachel, *this will keep my mind off my troubles.*

Marion glanced across at Rachel. "I can see you believe nothing of what I've just told you."

"You see clearly. I do not believe a word, amazing as your story is. But I'm used to amazing stories. I was raised on remarkable tales and don't believe them either."

"Oh really? Like what?"

"I was born in Zion, here in Illinois," said Rachel.

Marion shook her head. "Never heard of it."

"You should have if you were really alive back in the day. The town reached its zenith in the early twentieth century, when you claim you were already born."

CHAPTER THIRTEEN

The Reverend John Dowie, self-proclaimed faith healer, fled arson charges after his well-insured Australian church burned to the ground in 1888. He packed his Bible and set sail for California, calling on God to heal the seasickness of his fellow passengers, with mixed success. His fortunes did not improve on the West Coast. He soon travelled East and set up shop in a shed outside the gates of the 1893 Chicago World's Fair. There his luck improved. He gained favor with several wealthy widows who bankrolled his vision of establishing a theocratic city on the shore of Lake Michigan. With their money, he purchased a swath of prime land just north of the city, which was no longer inhabited because the United States Army had forced the Potawatomi people West in the 1830s under the Federal Indian Removal Act.

John Dowie had charisma, no one could dispute that. He converted a prominent city planner to become a member of his flock and soon had in hand the plans for a new city. Zion, Illinois, opened for business in 1902, with every street named for a location in the Bible. Dowie's huge Tabernacle dominated the center of town, its entryway decorated with the finest crutches and braces the pawn shops of

Chicago had to offer—or castoffs of the cured, if you believed the church leaders. The town police were deputized to escort out of the city limits any physician who dared to set up shop in Zion. And even the revelation that Dowie himself consulted Chicago's finest doctors for his cancer could not sway the true believers in town. Dissolving the grip of the theocratic government happened decades later when Dowie's successor, Glen Voliva, confessed that he too had cancer, was consulting Chicago doctors, and was afraid of going to hell after bilking the congregants for years.

And so it was that a civic government took over city hall, and the classrooms of Zion stopped displaying maps of the flat earth, and the Bible disappeared from the city seal (with help from an ACLU lawsuit). Paved streets, indoor plumbing, and modern medicine came to town.

In the midst of that chaos, Rachel's mother Jenny grew up in Zion and remained a true believer. No wonder, then, that Jenny was afraid to expose her only child Rachel to the wicked institution that the Zion public schools had become.

In Rachel's early memories of her mother, Jenny was always praying. Jenny prayed for Rachel's dad to come back. She prayed for some benefactor to help them. She prayed for work. That last one came through. Jenny got a job in a law office in the next town. Working there was less sinful than working in a doctor's office, for doctors were the devil's helpers. Throughout her life, Jenny believed there were no such things as germs, and disease was punishment for sins. And she remained fully certain that the earth was flat.

Jenny's family had been early settlers in Zion. Her grandfather arrived as a young child in 1910, his parents convinced the aftereffects of his polio could be reversed by the laying on of hands, if only he would pray harder. The family lived through all the trials and tribulations of the church: the church-owned factories where congregants worked for a pittance, the church-owned newspaper that proclaimed the truth of faith healing, the church-owned radio station with its ceaseless claims of a flat earth. When the Second World War came, the able-bodied young men went off to fight and came back with new ideas, but Jenny's family didn't listen. When television arrived with a barrage of new information, Jenny's family turned it off.

But science came to Zion, ready or not, with the announcement of a nuclear power plant to be built in town, on the shore of Lake Michigan. Dirk Sutter arrived in 1965. He was a nuclear engineer, assigned to set up systems as the reactor was under construction. Jenny fell in love; Dirk fell in lust. Jenny was sure she could convert him to her faith; after all, he agreed to be wed in the church. Their daughter Rachel turned four the year the power plant opened. Dirk packed one suitcase, kissed his child goodbye, left for the next construction site, and never came back. Rachel would walk past the plant as a child and wonder if anyone working there remembered her dad. Jenny said she took after him. That's why Jenny wanted to homeschool Rachel: because she was afraid Rachel would grow up to like science, as Dirk did. Jenny decided her husband had left because scientists are in league with the devil and he needed to rejoin his coven. But as a single mom Jenny could not homeschool Rachel because Jenny had to work.

So naturally when Rachel earned top grades in high school science, she said nothing to her mother. When she got a scholarship to Northwestern and declared a biology major, Rachel kept as much as she could to herself. Even so, Jenny suspected the devil had taken her daughter.

Rachel loved being out in nature almost as much as she loved science. In grade school, her favorite trail led through the tall grasses on the shore of the lake and past the reactor. She wondered if her dad was kind or was more like her mom's scary new boyfriend. When she was ten her mother began to warn her off boys, not knowing that Rachel liked girls much better. Jenny warned Rachel off science, too, but it was too late. Rachel had already promised herself that she would only ever believe in what she could see or measure. No religion for Rachel, and certainly no vampires.

When Rachel was in middle school, the school nurse tested the students' vision and sent her to the county health clinic where they fitted her with a pair of someone's castoff glasses. They were close enough. The people at the clinic told her to stop reading books under the covers at night.

Rachel met a girl at the glasses clinic, and they turned out to be in science class together. They talked about their missing dads, wondered what they were like. When Rachel got home she told her mother that she had made a friend.

"Is she a good Christian, this friend?" Jenny asked.

"That's not what we talked about."

"What did you talk about?"

"Stuff." What could Rachel possibly tell her mother about her first crush?

Rachel's twelfth grade science teacher was a man, and the girls in class knew to only go see him in twos. They talked about how they were going to escape and go to university, but Rachel was the only one in her circle of friends who did.

She first heard about blood transfusions when she was in college. They tested each other's blood types in lab, and visited a blood bank where they learned about blood testing. They learned how many people's lives each year are saved by transfusions. Someone at the blood bank called their business "the science of moving life from one person to another." It sounded like a living chess game. Rachel was intrigued, but she did not get a blood bank job right away. Her first job out of college was inspecting hospitals for an accreditation board.

Then Rachel met Theresa, a lab tech at Chicago General Hospital. They met while Rachel was inspecting the hospital, back before Rachel joined FDA. Theresa was tall, and a serious nerd. And although she was a junior tech she ran circles around everyone else in her lab. Rachel went to interview the head of the lab and he brought in Theresa to answer questions. He pretended it was because he wanted to give her the opportunity; in reality, Theresa could answer better than he. He hid behind her and Theresa knew it. So did Rachel.

Rachel and Theresa kept in touch after the inspection. There were just a few follow-up questions for her lab, and somehow they managed to string out the correspondence until Rachel changed jobs and joined FDA. Then they could see each other with no conflicts of interest. Theresa moved up to run a testing lab at another hospital and Rachel moved up from junior to senior inspector for the agency. And the two of them moved in together.

The women were inseminated with the same donor at the same time. They expected that getting pregnant would take a while, but it took no time at all. People thought their children were twins because Theresa and Rachel gave birth within a week of each other, but biologically their babies were half-siblings. They were six when Theresa was killed in a car crash on her way home from work. From that day on, Rachel's life was about two things: the children and her career. But now the children were grown and working in Europe.

Rachel paused for a moment. "I decided I could not stand losing another partner. It was brutal. I'd rather be on my own. Plus I'm in my fifties now. Time to set aside thoughts of romance. Even if I weren't sick."

Marion smiled at that. "You're a young thing."

"If you say so. Anyway, back when I was at university, I was in class one day and the professor was explaining cells: how each part has a job. And the cells together make a tissue. And tissues together make an organ. And at each level new properties emerge. Unexpected, unexplained. And for a moment I saw life itself, its glory, its majesty. And that thing, that idea, of emergent properties, I realized must be what my mother talked about when she talked about the soul. And for a second I felt connected with my mother, as if love too were an emergent property, as if I had a soul and my mother had a soul and everything my mother had tried to instill in me was sort of, kind of, true.

"And then the professor said, 'This is what molecules do. This is what the universe does to understand itself. This gestalt, this life, this thing we have for a moment, until entropy takes over and we die.' The room was hushed. No one breathed. And in that moment I became an atheist. Or maybe a pantheist, I'm never quite sure of the difference. Any last little vestige of belief in the Bible ended that day." Rachel smiled. "The guy in the office next to mine has a sign on his door that says, 'In God We Trust. All Others Bring Data.' If I had a sign on my door, it would just say, 'Bring Data.'"

Marion nodded. "And now this blood bank president is asking you to believe something so outlandish, it makes the stories in the Bible look like real estate listings."

Rachel threw up her hands. "Yes! You expect me to believe this crazy story? That you're not human, not even alive? You don't understand who you're dealing with. I do not believe in life after death. I do not believe in the Resurrection. Certainly not the resurrection of a blood bank owner in a backwater town."

Marion picked up a scalpel from a lab bench. Rachel flinched, wondering if it were intended for her. *Relax*, she told herself. *You're dying anyway. What do a few months matter?*

"You want data?" Marion brought the scalpel down straight into the palm of her left hand, then pulled it out again. She held it up for Rachel to see. No blood. And the cut had sealed instantly, leaving no trace.

"Want me to validate this? How many tries will make it statistically valid? Ten?" Marion switched hands and brought the scalpel down into her other hand, then held it up while the wound sealed, bloodless.

"How about this? Eh?" She pulled up her sleeve and stabbed her arm. It sealed. "Other arm? Just so?" Marion pulled up that sleeve and stabbed. Sealed again.

"Alright! Enough." Rachel's mind was turning over possibilities, rapidly. Nothing seemed to explain what she saw, at least nothing biological. "Are you trained as a magician?"

"No. And if I were, how would I fake this? A retractable knife would not leave a wound. Here." She handed the scalpel to Rachel. "Your turn."

"No. No, I won't."

"Just do it. Otherwise you won't believe me."

Rachel looked Marion in the eye while she stabbed her arm. She felt the point go into Marion's flesh. Rachel looked down, expecting blood.

Not one drop.

"There you have it," said Marion. "Data."

RECONNECTIONS 2010

CHAPTER FOURTEEN

"You must believe me, Rachel. We only want to live, and to live without hurting others."

"And when you say that '*we* only want to live,' who is the 'we?' Who else do you mean, besides you?"

"I mean the Sisters of the Night, whom I met as a young woman in York, who are now the night shift here at the Blood Bank."

"Other vampires?"

"Yes."

"Your entire night shift consists of medieval vampires." Rachel could not believe she was saying these words.

"That's right."

"Everybody working in this basement."

"Yes."

"How did that happen?"

"Social media is a great way to find people you've lost track of."

"Sure," said Rachel. "Like old high school sweethearts."

"And immortals you knew in the fifteen hundreds."

With an effort, Rachel kept a straight face. "Do tell."

~

When the First World War broke out, Marion became a nurse with the Prairie Division out of Illinois. Zinc oxide sunblock made it easier for Marion to travel. When she crossed the Atlantic, she could stand on deck in the daytime and gaze at the blue ocean. She wore sunglasses newly developed to protect the sensitive eyes of syphilis patients, which worked very well for vampires too.

As with past wars, the Great War gave Marion many opportunities to heal, some of them unexpected. One night she stood in a trench during a mustard gas attack. Marion had already discovered that gas attacks did not affect her, and she wore a gas mask only to prevent questions. The soldier standing beside her was in increasing distress because his mask failed, and Marion quickly swapped masks with him. As his breathing returned to normal, the young man turned to her and said, "What manner of angel are you, that my broken mask protects you?"

Marion smiled under her gas mask. "I'm not sure 'angel' is the right word, Soldier," she said.

A month later, while tending to victims of explosions, Marion met Percy Lane Oliver, an Englishman who worked for the Red Cross. He told her about his plans to open a blood donation center in London once the cruel war was over—a plan that interested Marion greatly. "And when the blood is too old, what will you do with it?"

"We will dispose of it, of course," said Percy.

"What a waste," said Marion, although she knew Percy would not understand.

Marion was already interested in the field of blood transfusions, but the concept of an organized blood bank gave her ideas for a new way to feed herself and others like her. Blood transfusions, blood donation, blood banking, all became the focus of her work. When the war ended, it was time to hang up her nurse's cap and try something new. After the war she returned to Chicago, where, with Marion's help, Bernard Fantus opened the first blood bank in 1937.

Marion kept a low profile in the early years of blood banking. But she was there to guide research in directions that benefitted both mortals and vampires. For example, she made sure that the anticoagulants adopted to preserve blood did not interfere with vampire digestion. Marion's personal needs were simple: just a place underground to sleep in the day and lab space at night. Meanwhile her fortune, the result of various liaisons, continued to grow, managed by a firm of pragmatic European bankers who did not question why the same person kept depositing funds for centuries. Finally, in 2009, when Marion had risen through the ranks of a blood bank near Chicago, she decided to use some of her money to buy the business and run it as she chose.

The year Marion bought the Lake County Blood Bank, she hardly had time to socialize. But with her sleep schedule so disrupted by working in the daytime, she sometimes logged onto her computer at odd hours and checked out social media. *Strange phrase, social media,* she mused, *for something so totally anti-social.* Especially when she logged on late at night and found herself in the company of some quite unusual characters. There were sufferers from rare diseases, people with strange fixations, and the ever-present kinky folk. *But then,* she thought, *who am I to call anyone odd?*

Along with the misfits and belligerents she began to see hints of her own kind. Names like "Late Night Wanderer" and "Lady Vamp" could mean tiresome vampire wannabes, romanticizing a life they knew nothing about. Or was this electronic medium a way to connect with her ancient Sisters? Marion's internet scrolling grew more systematic as she searched sites and groups that looked promising. Her own screen name was Bloodborn—just as phony-sounding as any of the others online. And then one night Marion received a message from someone called Blood Sister.

"Are you who I think you are? Tell me where you met Anna Marshall."

Marion was intrigued. "And who are you?"

Blood Sister typed, "Tell me. How did you meet Anna?"

"I met her at the Shambles in York."

"And what was she doing?"

"She was a prostitute."

"And what did you do?"

"I tried and failed to save her." *How strange,* thought Marion, *to be typing these words on her computer.*

"Aha! Is this Marion?"

"First tell me: Who are you?"

"This is Sarah Clarke, from Camden House long ago."

"Sarah! Where are you now?"

"I'm in Scotland. Not thriving. I tire of rodents. Are you really Marion? Where are you?"

"Yes! Sarah! I'm in America. I just bought a blood bank. You should come here."

"A blood bank. Brilliant! No more rats for you?"

"Once in a while, for old time's sake. Come to Chicago. Fly at night. And bring sunscreen, just in case."

Sarah laughed. "I always do. And when did you go to America?"

"In 1862," said Marion. "Pre-sunscreen. I stayed below decks, ate every rat, and by the time we docked, I could have bled a horse dry."

Sarah found Sybil, and Sybil found Lillian. Lillian found Gwen, and Gwen found Alice. And so it began: The gathering of the Sisters and the beginnings of the night shift at the Lake County Blood Bank. As they contacted each woman, Marion explained her plan to harvest human blood for them, ethically, at the blood bank. She found a medical technology school where the Sisters could complete their coursework at night and be certified as lab technicians. Not surprisingly, the women were avid students.

All told, they gathered eleven of the twelve Sisters from Camden House—everyone except Kate. Perhaps Kate was never online; perhaps she had lived a short life, for a vampire. There was no way to know.

SUNSCREEN

CHAPTER FIFTEEN

"So where do you sleep?" Rachel asked, suspending her disbelief for the moment.

"Right here in the basement. Each of us has a little room. Spartan, but bigger than coffins."

Rachel had slipped through the looking glass: First that horrible call from her doctor, and now she was having a lucid conversation with a madwoman. And she had been lusting after this madwoman until today. It made her headache worse. Still she continued the conversation. "As a vampire, how is it that you can work in daylight?"

"First, the blood bank has no windows."

"Yes, I've noticed. The place is sealed like a crypt."

Marion sighed. "How droll."

"Sorry."

"And I use a sun block when I'm upstairs in daylight. It's much better than the cream I invented a couple hundred years ago—the modern version contains nanoparticles of zinc oxide. It doesn't turn your skin white, but still does the job. Plus I have Amber to assist me. She can go out into direct sunlight no problem, because she is mortal."

"So that's why you sent Amber up to the roof, instead of going yourself."

"Indeed. I'd be happy to go up there at night if you want to see it again."

"But wait—did you say that you invented sunscreen?"

"I improved it. The ancient Romans actually invented it. I'm not *that* old." Marion smiled at this. Rachel did not smile back.

Marion looked into the distance, willing the memories to come. "My work on sunscreen began in the war."

"Which war?"

"Which, indeed. There were too many."

Marion saw that war, horrible as it was, was a great gift to her kind. Working as a night nurse, she became the angel of men who were dying painful deaths with no hope of recovery. She would sit at a man's bedside, soothing his brow with damp cloths, and listen to his cries. As she watched the doctors work, she learned the limits of their skills and came to know which men were destined to die. Each night she would wait until the lights were out and no one was able to see her give peace to some suffering man. Her only wish was that the Sisters of the Night could join her, because she alone had no appetite for the vast amount of blood shed by the men who were grievously wounded in war.

For years after she left York, Marion traveled from one bloody battle to the next. When men were so determined to let each other's blood, her small harvest went unnoticed.

This profession of nursing seemed to Marion the middle ground between saint and sinner that her friend Vivienne had once wished for. Where was Vivienne now? Marion longed for someone to share the horrors she witnessed. Were her Sisters Alice and Paulina still nurses, somewhere? There was sustenance aplenty in these killing grounds, but it was a ghastly business.

And so Marion wandered across the battlefields of Europe and finally across the vast Atlantic to the United States. She arrived soon after the start of the Civil War and found that her skills in nursing were most welcome. Here the carnage was so great that doctors, far from feeling threatened by the expertise of women nurses, were relieved to have any help at all. Marion held down men who were having limbs amputated. She administered the few medicines that were available. She bathed the men and changed their dressings. And as before, she sat with the dying.

Marion's first glimpse of a Civil War hospital tent, lit by just a few candles to minimize the chance of an enemy attack, was like watching hog butchering by candlelight. The doctors moved from man to man, deciding quickly where to spend their efforts, while the men on endless stretchers tried their best to hold back their moans. Blood was everywhere, so much blood that instead of stimulating her hunger it made her sick to see it. In her white hospital apron and starched hat, Marion stood out as a new arrival, but not for long. She was pulled into service to hold down a man while a doctor severed his leg and then directed Marion to cauterize the man's bleeding when he was finished. Marion did as she was told. Even in her mortal existence she could have restrained this man, so weak was he from wounds and lost blood. She soon mastered the use of the cautery, a heated metal rod essential to burn the end of a severed limb and prevent the amputee from bleeding to death. The smell of cooked human flesh made her gag; she, who had bled men and rats to death and who thought that nothing could reach her, was sickened and appalled by the scope of the carnage. The few doctors creeping their way from cot to cot could do almost nothing, faced with the enormity of the need.

When the war ended in April of 1865, the makeshift war hospital gradually closed down and Marion shifted to a rehabilitation hospital in Atlanta that treated the long-term injuries of the war wounded. One early morning in October she finished her nursing shift while it was still dark and found her way to the basement of a ruined house where she sometimes rested. The basement was surprisingly neat, and not infested by any rat or other vermin—she herself had seen to that. And there she would have stayed, asleep, until nightfall, except that something awakened her mid-afternoon. She rose and made her way toward the stairs to the surface, feeling her way because there was no light.

No light, in the afternoon. Why not?

At the doorway she saw people staring upward, mouths agape. The sounds of city life were dimmed as people all over town gazed at a sky full of stars at midday. The sun was gone from the sky, obliterated by the first full eclipse Marion had seen in her long life.

For Marion, the sight of the city, dimly lit by the faintest edge of corona, was as alien as the light of unfamiliar constellations. She wondered at the new knowledge that awakened her to this ghost light, annoyed once again that there was so much to learn about her condition and no one to teach her. And at the same time, standing outside in midafternoon, however bizarre an afternoon, filled her with the desire to stand in sunlight again. Marion carried that longing with her as the eclipse continued, the threatened rays of sunlight chasing her back into the depths of the earth. She must stand in the light again, and she would not die doing it. The only question was how to make that happen.

As a first step, Marion took on a new identity. She became Gerald Parker the chemist, and regained the freedom she had known long ago dressed as a man, when she was the bawd at Camden House. She visited colleges near Atlanta, hoping to secure access to a library and a research laboratory, but the schools in the South had been shattered by war. All she found were a few drunken sons of the old aristocracy who wagered and fought in the broken buildings. Not finding what she needed in the ruins of the Confederacy, Marion travelled north to Chicago, where she apprenticed herself to a pharmacist and worked at night, compounding prescriptions for morning delivery and conducting her own research in the off hours.

It was a precarious existence; she could not reveal her gender to anyone, much less her true nature as a vampire. But Marion had lived alone in her cottage for many years and was fond of her own company, especially now that she had a project that compelled her. She had not felt this driven since she crafted remedies in her cottage at Whixton.

More devastation followed when the Great Chicago Fire consumed much of the city. Fortunately Marion's pharmacy was spared. Then in a show of sympathy, the British Parliament organized a donation of eight thousand books to found the Chicago Public Library. Once its doors were opened, Marion spent many an evening there, researching her project. She believed that for her kind to be safe by day, they needed a covering that reflected sunlight, not just absorbed it. As she read natural philosophy in the new library, she was drawn to the writings of the ancient Romans, who had discovered this reflective property in a derivative of zinc. Marion hoped that zinc oxide would protect her kind from the ravages of sunlight. She obtained some of the thick white material and mixed it with the herbals she had on hand in this New World: aloe vera, and mushroom extract, and oil of primrose. It seemed like this cream would be effective, but how to test it? If she covered her little finger and exposed only that to the sun, could she tell if it worked? And if it did not, would she lose just that finger? Or would her whole body turn into ash?

Marion continued her research, dressed as a man, for years, frequenting salons in Chicago where natural philosophy was discussed. It was at such a gathering that she met Walter Cobb.

He drew her aside and said, "Tell me, my dear, how long have you posed as a man?"

"I am amazed, Sir, that you choose to be so forward. Are your passions so unnatural and are you so brazen?"

"What is unnatural is that a woman must make a pretense to be accepted here as an equal. It is clear that you are more than equal to any man, regardless of your sex."

Marion reflected that her passion for Cecily had been deemed unnatural, and she regretted using such language now to defend herself from being unmasked. But this man spoke quietly; if his intent had been to ruin her, he could easily have done so already.

He beckoned. "Come. Let us walk outside and discuss another way than the wearing of false garments."

Once on the well-kept grounds behind the meeting hall, she spoke more freely.

"I do not think of these garments as false, Sir. In fact I look forward to the day when women can appear in public in pants and shirts, without fear of approbation. What seems false to me are the corsets and high heeled shoes that limit our stamina and our movement."

"Agreed. And yet you risk exposure each time you dress in men's clothing, especially in a gathering that is closed to women. It is a conundrum, I grant you. I anticipate the day it all changes, though not in our lifetime, I fear."

Not in yours, perhaps, was Marion's uncharitable thought. "And what do you suggest instead?"

"Come live with me. Be, to all appearances, my mistress, though I will expect no favors of that kind from you. Send me to every meeting of the Natural Philosophers that interests you, and I will bring home every philosopher you wish to meet. We will set up a salon, an informal gathering once a month, open to both men and women, where you may appear in your rightful guise and learn everything you wish to learn, spin your own theories and prognostications. The world is changing. Let us begin to change the view of society about women philosophers."

She stared. "And why would you do that for me, someone you only met tonight?"

He smiled. "I have seen you before at these gatherings, always in the back, never daring to speak out for fear of being identified. I've seen how you chafe in that role, especially when a questionable proposition demands a pointed response that no one else is making. We cannot change these staid old groups, at least not in an instant. But we can create our own."

She said, "If I were not dressed as a man, I would kiss you now."

Walter had been a merchant in the Chicago livestock trade, had sold his company for a great gain in his sixtieth year. He was intent on enjoying his remaining years to the hilt. Marion moved into his elegant Lake Forest home where she had her own apartments and her own laboratory, in a separate building in the back that reminded her of her cottage in the woods long ago. Walter was not, of course, her senior, but she seemed almost like a daughter to him. He fussed when she would not eat, and so she pretended at times to do so. He was infatuated with her despite what appeared to be their age difference. She came to enjoy lying with him, though she never felt the passion she had experienced with Cecily so long before. When brigands set upon their carriage one night as it drove down a country lane, Walter called upon the driver, but it was Marion who took the guns from the robbers, stripped them of their clothes, and sent them naked out onto the prairie. Walter never asked her how one woman could overcome them, and the carriage driver stayed silent on the matter.

Their salon was a great success. Not only did philosophical men come to call, but as requested, they brought their wives and mistresses, some of whom were philosophers as well. And as word spread other women came, some with men, others in the company of women.

At one of the salons, Marion discussed her experiments with sun lotion, as she called it.

One man asked, "But why would a woman want such a thing? Aren't you taught to avoid the sun, to keep your pale complexion?"

"Perhaps we wish for the freedom men enjoy, to travel freely outside, without fear of compromising ourselves by our appearance."

"Are you not already compromised, by living with a man to whom you are not wed?"

Walter took him aside and let him know that such talk was not welcome in his house. That night when everyone had left, Walter asked Marion to marry him. That was their last salon before Walter fell into his final illness.

When her lover Walter fell ill with a wasting disease, a disease that Marion could not cure, try as she might, all she could do was make him comfortable with potions that eased his pain. He finally said to her one night, "Even with all you do for me, my dear, I cannot abide this life. It is time." She was crying then, not only because he was dying, but because she could not give him life eternal. It was against her moral code and the code of her Sisters to grant any man eternal life. He was going to die, and she was not going to stop it.

"Give me peace, my darling," he said. "Give me a draught that will end my pain, not just for a little while, but for always."

She kissed him goodbye, she gave him a potion, and as he slept, she drank his blood. It was the first human blood she had taken since the war. Oh Goddess it tasted good.

But her husband's blood did not sate her for long. One night as she caught a rat near the laboratory to make a meager meal, Marion wondered whether a rat could tell her what she needed to know about her zinc lotion. Could she create a rat vampire? And if she did, how would it fare in daylight? She resolved to try.

She took in all the blood the rat had to offer and then, shivering at the thought of what she had to do, Marion bit her own wrist and extended it to the rat. As the rat drank at her wrist she saw scenes she would never forget and that even she, inured to horror as her life as a vampire had made her, was loath to experience. Rats devouring one another, live, in stinking alleyways. Rats covered head to toe in fleas. Rats eating human waste, or eating garbage so foul she teetered on the edge of pulling her wrist away so that she could retch. But fortunately, the rat had a small stomach and took little of her blood. She locked the vile creature in a box awaiting the dawn.

Just before sunrise, she took the rat, now much stronger than a mortal rodent, and tied it to a cart outside so that it would be exposed to the sun's rays. The rat twisted and tried to get away, but as strong as it now was, Marion was stronger still.

She absented herself into her house where, covered in her new lotion and sheltered from the sun's rays, she waited for some sign of what happened. But there was no sound, and instead she crept into the basement to wait for dark to come again. At nightfall Marion emerged to find a small pile of ash at the end of the rope, a miniature version of the ashes left by Anna's departure.

That night Marion repeated the same sorry ritual of turning a caught rat into one of her own fellow creatures. This time she covered the rat in the zinc paste she had created. It looked strange, as if its fur had been painted white. As morning approached she once again tied a preternaturally strong rat to the cart in front of her laboratory. There were no ashes that night; instead, the rat had eaten through the rope and run away.

Days later she heard rumors of a vicious rat in the neighborhood that drained the blood of its fellows. That rat was chopped to bits by the father of a baby it attacked in its crib. But Marion had created what she was looking for: a way to protect herself and her fellow creatures from dying in sunlight. If only she could find her Sisters once again to tell them.

Dressed in a wide brimmed hat and covered head to toe in her own concoction, Marion saw sunlight for the first time in years. It was a gray day in winter. Trees were bare and clouds obscured the full glory of day. But for Marion, closeted in darkness for centuries, the aspect was thrilling beyond words. She marveled at the pale shadows cast by the half-light. She was in awe of crows circling overhead, of carriages seen in color for the first time. It had been so long that she had forgotten the shades visible in a horse's coat, forgotten the green of an oak tree in daylight. Seeing all that was as memorable as the night she was first made a vampire and saw the stars in their true glory.

Now a wealthy widow, and with the patent on zinc oxide sun lotion in hand, Marion made use of her dead husband's wardrobe and joined the early research into blood transfusions in Chicago.

The blood of dying soldiers. Rampaging rats. And here in the basement of the blood bank, blood used for food in the fridge. The cell-like dormitories, which were palaces compared with the coffins they were used to. The research—surely doomed—to develop synthetic blood to feed their crazed appetites. Rachel must be having a nightmare where everything about her orderly world had gone bizarrely cracked. It was enough to make her feel faint.

"Are you alright?"

"No. You know I'm not."

"If the treatments don't work, there is another way."

"Oh really?" Rachel waved her arms. "Does it involve hocus-pocus? Horned devils? Stinking ghouls?"

"No. It involves love."

Rachel stood up and took out her cell phone.

"What are you doing?"

"I'm calling headquarters in DC. My district office can't handle this. We need backup."

"You're calling in the guys with the guns? The ones who take company presidents away in handcuffs?"

Rachel held up one hand for Marion to be quiet. Then she put her hand on her forehead; suddenly she had a blazing headache. "Yes," she said on the phone. "Get me Enforcement. This is—"

But before she could say her name, everything went dark. Was it her illness? Or was Marion stopping her from getting help?

Strong woman's arms caught her as she fell.

LUKE PAYS A VISIT
CHAPTER SIXTEEN

Amber and Luke had a tense day. Together once again in the archive room, where they had enjoyed each other's company in past days, the two barely spoke. But they could not stay focused on business. Amber finally interrupted their stone-faced exchange of documents.

"I know you don't really want me to go to jail."

"And I know you have a lover. I saw you with some long-haired guy outside the diner."

That explained a lot.

Maybe, thought Amber, she was a bit circumspect when she described Gregory to Luke simply as a rock-and-roll guitar player who loved her exactly as she was right now and didn't want her to change. But she could hardly say more. "And, by the way," she added, "I've broken it off with Greg."

Luke chuckled. "How convenient, now that you know I've seen you together."

"No, I really did."

For all the skeptical air that Luke put on, he was filled with relief. He wanted so much to believe that Amber was through with that man. He wanted so much to kiss her. And he wanted so much to shake some sense into her. Was she stuck in some adolescent groupie time-warp?

"What do you want, Amber? What kind of life? Do you want children? A stable home life?"

She shrugged. "Sure. Sure I want those things."

"You don't sound sure."

"But I want other things too. Excitement. Loud music. Dancing."

"You want day and night."

"Yes. Exactly."

"The best relationships have both, you know."

Amber laughed. "And how do they achieve that, pray tell?"

"Well…"

"Really, Luke, how many people do you know who have relationships with all that? Cozy, plus fireworks?"

It was Luke's turn to laugh. "You have a point. I'm not sure, actually. I mean, how do you know what people are like behind closed doors?"

"Exactly. And if you get your ideas about romance from the movies, guess what? Real life is not the Director's Cut of the latest romcom."

"I know that," he said, and as he did, he reached across the table and stroked her arm, making her shiver.

"Don't do that." She jerked her arm back.

He pulled back his hand and sat up straight. "I want to believe it's possible to want what you actually have."

"And how would that happen?"

"Here, stand up. Let me show you." He had nothing to lose; Amber had just broken up with that greasy fake, and this was his chance, before she found another nasty character.

Amber stood, arms crossed, and Luke stood facing her. "Here's my idea of how people keep love alive. Uncross your arms. Please."

She did, and he put his hands on her shoulders. "They take turns feeling safe and not-so-safe. There is security…" Luke took her in his arms, held her close but gently.

Then he ran his fingers down her spine. "And there is excitement.

And you deserve it all." He was kissing her cheek as he said this, nuzzling her ear with his nose. She felt his human breath on her neck.

It felt to her like home, and a trip to the stars, all at once. "I see what you mean," she said. "But you do realize that someone could walk in here any minute, Inspector."

"Right," he said, and let go of her, resuming the awkward stance that Amber found so endearing.

They decided to take a break and walk down to the coffee room. He held her hand, just until they left the room, feeling extravagantly lucky. She was so small, he thought. So round and perfect like a Fabergé egg. Ginger and light and... what was the word? Effervescent. She effervesced through life. On a whim, he opened the door of the supply closet and beckoned her inside. She hesitated just for a moment, then came in and closed the door. Her scent was all around him, his arms were all around her. Her hair under his hands was smooth as cornsilk and as he embraced her she felt to him like the most perfect being who ever was. His lips found hers, and hers were soft, giving, and he pulled her close, his eyes closed, his body curved slightly to accommodate her shorter stature. His hands slipped under the back of her blouse and now he felt the skin of her back, just as smooth. He could barely believe that he got to hold her, and kiss her, and—just then he opened his eyes for a moment, and with his eyes now adjusted to the darkness he saw a line of light underneath the top shelf of the supply cabinet.

He stopped kissing her. "What is that?" He let go of her.

"What is what?"

"That light. Very dim, just there. That line of light, across the bottom of this shelf."

"I don't see a light."

"No, you wouldn't. It's above that shelf that's over your head. I think there's a door here."

"Oh! No, there can't be. You've seen the floorplans."

"Yes, of course." The floorplans. The ones that failed to show the extra air vents. The air vents that could serve an undisclosed basement.

"You are so lovely," he said, resuming his caresses.

"Thank you," she said. "You're not bad yourself."

"We should probably go, though, before things get out of hand."

"Aren't they already?"

He chuckled. "Not as much as they could be. Come, let me walk you to your car."

They walked to the front door, closer than two people should be who were only acquaintances, but not arm in arm, just in case they met someone.

He held the front door open for her. "Where are you parked?"

"Right here."

"I'll say goodnight, then." He kissed her, still holding the door open. "Mind if I go back in? Just need to visit the men's room for a second."

She hesitated. She could hardly demand to accompany him into the men's room, and how odd it would be to insist on protocol when they had just kissed.

"I'll come right back out, I promise," he said. "No bodyguard needed."

She laughed. "See you tomorrow."

"See you then." He waved as she drove away, then turned and headed back to the closet.

There had to be a latch somewhere.

And there was.

At the base of the stairs Luke found a deserted lab. He could hear voices, maybe women's voices, from behind a closed door. But he was drawn to a bank of glass-fronted refrigerators full of blood bags. He took out a bag. It was marked expired, but if it was expired, why refrigerate it? And the collection date indicated that it was still viable for another two weeks. Clearly they planned to use it, but for what?

He checked a few other bags. Some were expired but still viable, like the first bag. Some were marked rejects because they had tested positive for HIV or hepatitis. Were these people selling contaminated blood?

He passed the door of the conference room where the women's voices were coming from. Then he opened a different door that led to a back corridor. This part of the basement did not look like a blood bank or a lab. The hallway was painted beige and had closed doors on either side, spaced every ten feet or so. If there were rooms on the other side, they were small. Luke had never seen anything like it in a blood bank. He could not imagine what these rooms were for.

One door was open near the end of the hall, and he was startled to see that it was a bedroom. Small and sparely furnished, with a single bed, a small desk and chair, and a wardrobe. Like a monk's cell, except it had no window. Even a monk would have a window.

"May I help you?" A woman was folding laundry by the wardrobe. She was dressed in ordinary clothes, not lab clothes. "It's my day off, but if I can answer any questions..."

"Yes, just one: what is this place?"

Softly she walked over and stood face to face with him. "It's our refuge," she said, "from those such as you."

"What do you mean, those such as me?"

She smiled then, a very toothy smile. "Why, FDA inspectors, of course. What did you think I meant?"

"I was not sure. But why sleep down here? In this little place with no windows? Don't you have homes?" Luke recalled something he had read about a diagnostics company that brought in scientists illegally, refugees, asylum seekers, and exploited them, made them sleep in the lab, didn't pay them, only gave them food. "Are you from another country? Did you come here seeking asylum? Are you kept here against your will? We can help you."

She laughed. "I did come here from another country. We all did."

"Did you come here with papers?"

"I'm not sure what you mean."

"So you came to this country undocumented, and now you're forced to sleep in an underground room without windows?"

She shrugged. "These rooms are better than the alternative."

They were threatening her. He knew it. "I'll save you. I'll get you out of here."

She lifted his arm and pushed back his sleeve, then nibbled the inside of his forearm with her teeth. Every hair on Luke's body stood on end and he was gripped with the sense that ice ran through his veins. *Why?* He asked himself. *You're a foot taller than this woman. How could she possibly hurt you?*

She looked up at him then, still holding his wrist. "You have the wrong end of the telescope, my friend. If you stay down here too long, you are the one who will need to be saved."

He ran back toward the stairs. He had to find Rachel. Rachel would know what to do. He rehearsed what he would say.

They're hiding something at the blood bank, Chief. Something big. There is a whole floor of the building they did not show us on the tour. There's a basement lab. And not only that: Living quarters. And storage for blood. Blood that's older than the blood upstairs. Five or six weeks old, past the expiry set by the blood bank, but still useable. And they save blood that's contaminated.

Rachel, we're dealing with something very strange here. I'm not sure the night shift is human. I met this woman downstairs. It was her day off and she was folding her laundry. She had a tiny bedroom, like a cell. She said her name was Sybil. She said they swap out fake blood for rejected blood and send the fake blood to be destroyed. It's worse than we thought.

So far so good. But how could he tell Rachel this next part?

Sybil said they are vampires. The whole night shift. She said they were ethical vampires, committed to consuming human blood that is unfit for transfusions.

Crazy stuff. There had to be a rational explanation. Rachel would help him figure it out.

Just then he passed the conference room door that had been closed earlier. Now it was open. He glanced over and saw a woman passed out on the floor, another woman leaning over her.

The woman on the ground was Rachel. She had found the basement too. And Marion stood over her.

"What have you done to her?" Luke demanded, his fists clenched, rushing at Marion. "Rachel tried to turn you in, didn't she? So you attacked her! You demon! What have you done?"

"I didn't do anything to—"

"I know what's going on. Don't pretend, don't lie to me. I met one of your minions. It was her day off, she said. 'Leave now before I drain you dry,' she said. Monsters! You're all monsters!"

"Sit down, Luke. Sit DOWN." This last uttered in the command voice Marion had learned over the centuries. Luke sat on the chair from which Rachel had fallen.

He said, more quietly, "Was she calling Washington? Trying to turn you in? Is that why you hurt her?"

"Luke, Rachel has cancer. And she's taken a turn for the worse. I've called an ambulance."

"You're lying. You're making this up."

But now Luke could hear an ambulance siren growing louder.

"Go upstairs, Luke. Show them the way."

"They'll see your precious hidden basement."

Marion shrugged. "Just go, Luke."

Amber had parked at the far corner of the lot, unsure if she should stay or go. Why was Luke intent on returning to the building without her? Did he really go to the restroom? Or was he heading for the supply closet, in which case she should have stopped him?

And then she heard an ambulance coming their way. Was Luke sick? Had something happened to him?

Amber jumped out of the car and ran to the front door as the ambulance approached. There was Luke, just inside the door, holding it open.

"Are you alright? What's happened?"

"It's Rachel. She's collapsed in the basement. I need to show the paramedics the way."

"She's in the—How did she get there?"

Luke looked her in the eye. "Same way everybody does. Through the supply closet."

Amber could barely take in that Rachel had collapsed. But this? "You betrayed my trust in you. You went behind my back and invaded our space." She shoved him and he fell back, startled.

"Now, that is rich. You hid an entire floor of your operation from an FDA inspection. And hid what you do there. My God! What is it you do there? And this time I want the truth. No flirting. No evasions. Are you selling contaminated blood? Just tell me."

The ambulance pulled up, the siren drowning out the last of Luke's words. The paramedics brought out the gurney. More conversation would have to wait.

~

The paramedics loaded Rachel onto the gurney to carry her up the steps. Marion spoke to them. "Thanks for coming so quickly. Rachel has metastatic breast cancer. It's reached her liver, maybe her brain. She collapsed ten minutes ago. Possible stroke."

"And you are—"

"A friend."

"Come with us. You can tell us more in the ambulance."

Amber still had car keys in her hand. "Luke, ride with me. You should not be driving."

ABIGAIL STAFFORD HOSPITAL

CHAPTER SEVENTEEN

When Rachel regained consciousness she was in the emergency room surrounded by medical staff. And Marion.

"No! Not her! She hurt me! Send her away!" Rachel tried to rise but could not. The stricken expression on Marion's face meant nothing to her.

A male nurse took Marion's arm. "I'm sorry. We need her to be calm. I'll show you to the visitor lounge."

But Marion did not want to leave. She knew by now that no doctor could save Rachel. Only she could do that.

Marion allowed the nurse to walk her to a room set aside for relatives of Emergency Room patients. It was the kind of room she expected: The residual scent of bleach, a stained plaid couch and a couple of orange plastic chairs. Medical magazines on two cheap end tables completed the effect. How would she get back to see Rachel? She could force her way in, of course. But to do so would break every rule of the Sisterhood. There had to be a better way.

She waited, fuming, until a doctor came to speak with her.

"Your friend's cancer has reached her brain," he said. "I'm very sorry, but the cancer has induced a stroke. We're trying to control it. We're doing all we can but she may not last the night. When she is stabilized we will let you come sit with her. Her illness is not your fault, and you mustn't blame yourself, regardless of what she said to you. She was not thinking clearly. It was the cancer in her brain that made her say those things."

"Thank you, Doctor." Wait. She had only to wait. She was not good at waiting.

Luke stormed into the room with Amber behind him.

Marion held up one hand. "Luke, I did nothing to Rachel, except to make sure she reached the hospital to care for her cancer."

"Cancer! She doesn't have—"

"Listen to me. The doctor will be back soon and he can tell you what he just told me: That the cancer spread more quickly than expected. That Rachel is having a stroke induced by the cancer in her brain. She was supposed to go in for treatment next Tuesday. But now they say she may not make it. I'm sorry, Luke."

"She would have told me. You're making this up, to save yourself. Rachel knows the truth about your blood bank. And so do I."

"No, I'm not making anything up. The other day when you and Amber came into the conference room, Rachel had just taken a call from her doctor back home, and the news was not good. Metastasis to multiple organs."

Luke sat, put his head in his hands and wiped at his tears. It was all too much. First that insane woman in the basement, and now this. When he collected himself he went to the nurse's station for a report, then came back, sat with crossed arms and looked at Marion. "Even if what you're saying is true, that doesn't excuse anything else going on in that hellhole of yours. Tell me what the devil you are up to."

Marion sighed. "A long time ago, a woman saved me from death."

"What kind of death?

"Two kinds. I was about to be killed by a mob, and I committed suicide."

"That makes no sense. Here you are."

"Here I am, five hundred years later."

"You're delusional."

"No. I'm undead."

"You're nuts. Like that woman in your basement. And if Rachel is too sick to call in the Feds I will do it."

"Listen to me, Luke. Rachel is dying. Do you care about her?"

"Of course, she's my friend. She's my mentor. She is why I'm here."

"Then let me help her. The doctors can't, not really. Her disease has progressed too quickly. Even if you're not ready to believe me, what do you have to lose? Luke, let me have some time with her. I can save her."

He shook his head. "Why would you do that?"

"Because I care about Rachel."

Just then a nurse came to take Marion back to sit with Rachel. Amber put her hand on Luke's arm. He shook it off.

"What really happened with you and that pretty boy rock star? Did you break up or was that another lie?"

"I'm done with Gregory. He wanted to turn me into a vampire."

"He's one too? Is nobody in this town actually alive?"

"There's you and me, Babe. We're both very much alive."

"Yes well. I thought Rachel was too, and now… the nurse told me that she might not make it until morning."

Luke tried to pull himself together. He was embarrassed that Amber and Marion had seen him cry. Amber put her arm around his shoulder. "I'm so sorry about your boss," she said.

"She's not just my boss." He gestured with his hands, still on the edge of tears. "She's my mentor. She's the person who gave me my career. Nobody else cared if I sank or swam. Rachel cared. Cares."

"This is a good hospital, Luke. I'm sure they are doing their best."

"But what if it's not enough? I hate the thought of her dying here, practically alone. Her kids are in Europe. And they haven't let me back there to see her."

"Marion is with her. She cares about Rachel a lot, you know."

"Yes, so she says. Maybe Rachel is just her next meal."

Amber shook her head. "Marion is good people. If she says she wants to help, she means it." Amber leaned over and kissed Luke on the lips.

"Hey," he said. "You know I can't give you what that guitar player could give you."

"What's that?"

"Immortality."

Amber scoffed. "If I wanted that, don't you think I'd already have it? Half the people I know are LD."

"LD?"

"Living Dead. 'LD' doesn't jangle people's nerves the way 'vampire' does."

"Only because they don't know what it means."

"Anyway, I might want to go immortal someday. And if I do, I'll ask one of my vampire friends to help me. But for now, and the foreseeable future, I enjoy being very much alive. Free to walk out in the sunshine. Free to have babies if I want them. Free to kiss the living without them worrying if I'm searching for an artery."

"That's admirable. I think."

She squeezed his arm. "I'm sorry I could not be honest with you before about the work we do. But now that you've found out so much, it's important that you have the whole picture. Marion bought the blood bank so that she could provide blood that was no longer good for mortal patients but could keep the vampires of Illinois alive. She calls it 'ethically sourced blood.'"

He grunted, almost a laugh. "What a mixed-up, upside-down world."

"Listen, Luke. If Rachel is as sick as they say, there is a way to help her. She will be different. She won't be able to go out in the sunlight without protection. She'll need a safe place to sleep in the day. And of course people will think she's dead, and you won't be able to tell them the truth. But in most ways she will be the same Rachel you've known."

"So, if I'm to believe all this—and whether I end up believing it depends on how Rachel comes through—then I need to understand the whole picture. How many people in Illinois are actually vampires? And who are those people in your hidden basement? What are they really doing there?"

"There's no census for vampires. But based on what we've seen, there are probably a few hundred in Illinois, working at all kinds of night jobs. Night nurses, watchmen, even rock-and-roll guitarists like my friend Gregory. Former friend. And the women in the basement are developing artificial blood, for humans and vampires."

Just then, Marion returned to the waiting room. It was time to make a plan.

Marion sat in one of the ugly orange chairs. "Listen, Luke. I know you've been shaken up tonight and a lot of things don't make sense right now. But there is a way to save Rachel, and we need your help."

"So what do you mean, *save* her? Just *how* would you do that?

"I can make Rachel immortal too."

Amber squeezed Luke's arm. "There are really only two choices: Do you want her to die tonight? Or would you rather she become an immortal?"

He held his head in his hands. There was no choice, not really. "Alright. What can I do to help?"

"You met Sybil downstairs tonight, yes?"

Luke shuddered. "Oh yes, I met her. She put her teeth on my arm. My God what a night."

Amber frowned. "I'm sorry about the way she behaved. She should know better and we will speak with her. But she did tell you the truth, and now you know: Our night shift at the blood bank are vampires. They feed on rejected and expired blood, not on the blood of innocent people."

"She was ready to feed on me."

"But she didn't. She knew better than that. There are rules."

"Alright. If you say so." Luke looked at Marion. "But how do I know Marion didn't hurt Rachel, the way that thing in the basement wanted to hurt me?"

"Luke, you spoke with the nurses. She has cancer, it metastasized to her brain and induced a stroke. If you were inspecting some other blood bank, Rachel would not have a chance."

Luke stood and left the lounge. He went to the nurses' desk and asked for an update.

The nurse at the station looked up from her computer screen. "She's your boss? I'm sorry. Are you ready say goodbye to her?"

"No, not yet. Just a minute."

While Luke was out of the room, Amber got on the phone. "Sybil? Your day off is cancelled. Come to Abigail Stafford Hospital, third floor. Bring Gwen with you. Arrive at Room 3247 in thirty minutes. Wear funeral staff clothing, and bring a body bag and a gurney."

Luke came back to the waiting room. "Alright. I apologize. I got an update from the nurse. She asked me if I was ready to say goodbye to Rachel."

"No apology needed, Luke. Just be ready to take the next step when the team arrives. Sybil and Gwen are coming to fetch Rachel's body."

"Dear God."

"Steady Luke. They'll know what to do. Rachel won't stay dead for long."

The nurses allowed Marion and Luke into Rachel's room, while Amber stood watch for Sybil and Gwen.

When the two women from the blood bank arrived, Luke came out to meet them. They were dressed in black and looked somber as they pushed a gurney. He recognized the woman from the basement, who came over and tried to shake his hand. "Luke, I see you remember me. Sybil. Sorry about earlier. That's just my way of flirting—didn't mean to scare you. Oh, and this is Gwen."

All Luke could manage was a nod.

Sybil continued. "Did Marion tell you the plan?"

"Yes, she did."

"And did it make sense?"

"Yes. I think so."

"Alright. Let's make it happen."

Meanwhile in her room, Rachel struggled for breath, the monitor over her head beeping more and more slowly. Marion pulled the curtain closed around the bed. She sat back down and took Rachel's hand in hers. Luke came in from the hallway to see Rachel alive one last time, and Marion spoke to him.

"Once it appears that Rachel has passed away, our team from the blood bank can take her body out and then I can save her, bring her back. Once her heart has stopped, we will need to move quickly. Do not be frightened by what you are about to see. All will be well."

Then Marion turned to Rachel.

"I know you can hear me, dear Rachel, even though I sound far away. You are very ill, but soon you will feel much better. It will be painful, briefly, but then you'll be fine. Be strong, my dear, the difficult part will not last."

Gwen pulled the fire alarm. Staff began loading patients to take them to a safe part of the hospital. Behind the curtain it appeared that Marion was hugging Rachel, but with her face awkwardly positioned at Rachel's neck. Luke shuddered to see how much it looked like Sybil with her mouth on his arm. But then it was worse. Much worse. Marion drew all the blood from Rachel's body, and as she did, Rachel's back arched in pain. Marion too was in pain. This was not the ecstasy of tasting healthy blood from a human victim, for Marion was taking in the cancer from Rachel's body. She shuddered as she drank, not in passion but with an overwhelming feeling of illness and horror.

The monitors were still beeping, out of sync with the fire alarm. Then the machines at Rachel's bedside registered zero pulse and zero respiration, and her own alarms went off. A nurse's aide opened the curtain around Rachel's bed, and Luke spoke up. "I'm afraid our friend is gone," he said. "Please see to the living patients."

"You all need to evacuate," she said.

"Will do."

"Leave the deceased here."

But Luke pointed to the women in black with the gurney at the door.

"They're from the funeral home in Rachel's advance directive. They'll take her," said Luke.

The aide nodded and turned away. She had bigger problems. Sybil and Gwen loaded Rachel into a body bag and onto the gurney and sped to the elevator. Marion, Luke and Amber followed them.

Amber turned off the fire alarm and the elevator doors opened.

"Just Marion and Rachel in this car," said Amber. "The rest of us will take the stairs."

Marion fought the effects of the cancer, her superior immune system capable of ridding her quickly of any illness. By the time they reached the elevator, her only concern was whether it had been too long to revive Rachel.

~

There was no time to spare.

Once in the elevator with Rachel's body on the gurney, Marion pressed the STOP button to suspend them between floors. She unzipped the body bag and exposed Rachel, so white, almost blue, and wholly drained of vital fluid. Was it possible to revive her? Marion could not bear to think otherwise. She bit a hole in her own wrist and held the gushing limb to Rachel's slack mouth.

"Come on, darling, drink," she said. "Take it. Take my blood."

Nothing happened.

She leaned down and kissed Rachel, soft and lovingly, and dripped a bit of blood into her mouth. "Please, Rachel. You can do this. Show me it's not too late."

Marion felt the softest lick on her skin. "Yes! That's it! Keep going." And in a moment Rachel's eyes opened wide and she stared at Marion as she pulled greedily on the other woman's wrist. Marion was almost overcome by sensation as every cell in her body cried out for oxygen. She gripped the edge of the gurney so tightly that she was able to stay standing, able to meet Rachel's gaze, even as she gasped in pain. And in spite of the pain, Marion was mesmerized by the pictures of Rachel's life that flashed before her eyes.

She was in a church where everyone praying aloud. But she, Rachel, skeptic that she was, could barely keep from giggling when the minister promised them life eternal.

If only Rachel knew then what she was about to find out.

When the elevator doors opened on the ground floor, the gurney was empty and two women stood, bloodstained, at the door.

Amber was waiting. "My God! You both look like you desperately need a doctor."

Marion put her arm around Rachel and led her from the elevator. "Quick, get us out of here before anyone sees us. A doctor is the last thing we need."

A NEW LIFE

CHAPTER EIGHTEEN

Rachel awoke on a single bed in a vacant staff bedroom in the basement of the blood bank, with blankets up to her armpits. She wore a flannel nightgown, a loaner from Sybil. Marion sat in a chair beside her.

"What happened?" She remembered only bits and pieces. An ambulance ride. Doctors and nurses hovering over her. Being inside a bag. Pain, all kinds of pain, cancer invading her body. More pain as her cells were starved for oxygen while the blood drained from her body.

"A lot happened. You were ill—very ill. Now you have a new life."

"I died?"

"Yes. You died."

It was too much. Rachel tried to stand up. "I need some air. I need to go outside."

"It's eight in the morning. If you walk out there right now, we won't need to cremate your body."

"What do you mean?"

"Let me tell you the new facts of life, my dear. The sun is no longer your friend."

"I can never go outside?"

"You can go out at night, any time you want. Daytime too—with a bit of planning. You'll need sunglasses, a scarf or a hat, and sunblock with zinc all over your body. Takes a bit of preparation, that's all. And you can't stay out too long, and you can't stay out if it rains, because if the sunblock rinses off, you're a cinder."

Rachel sat down heavily. "What else should I know?"

"There will be a false funeral, of course. You'll need to decide when or if you're going to tell your children that you are still alive, in altered form."

"God, that's right. And my job. If I'm dead that means I'm unemployed. And my pension? Gone. How do I make money?"

"You could run the night shift here at the blood bank. We could use a good manager."

"The night shift. I remember, they're all vampires, aren't they?"

"Every single one."

"What about Luke? Does he know?"

"Yes. Luke knows everything: that you're one of us now. That the blood bank feeds the undead, ethically, although maybe not in compliance with FDA regulations." Marion smiled.

Rachel was nowhere near ready to smile back. "I have to talk with him. I have to find out what he's going to tell the agency." Rachel squeezed Marion's hand. "You saved my life, didn't you?"

"Yes, I did. I should have asked you first, explained what you'd be getting into—but you were busy dying. I hope you don't mind that I took the liberty. This vampire business isn't all bad, you know. Got rid of your cancer. And you can't catch human diseases. On the other hand, although I'm well off after investing for hundreds of years, I still live hand to mouth, so to speak, when it comes to food. I can't just go buy a steak at the market. I have money in banks that few even know exist. I own jewels and mansions, but I can't drive through a fast food place for lunch." She patted Rachel's hand. "You've lost certain freedoms. If it's daytime you can't swim. You can't even go outside if it's raining. In fact, you can't wash your hands and then go out in daylight unless you reapply sunscreen. On the other hand, you're still alive. But the more you stick with nightlife the better."

Rachel was barely listening. "And all that business about being attracted to me. The kisses, the flirting. Was that just to win me over because I was inspecting your business? Because that's all over now."

"I understand. Give yourself a minute. This is a huge adjustment." Marion smiled again. "Becoming undead is a bigger deal than menopause."

Rachel had to smile back at that one. "You must be exaggerating."

"But when you're ready, let's see where this goes. I find you very intriguing, Dr. Sutter. The most interesting woman I've met in a hundred years."

Rachel restrained herself from reaching for Marion. She was right: best to give it some time. "You're the most interesting woman I've met in a hundred years too—or at least, as much of a hundred as I've been privileged to live."

"To live so far. You have many lifetimes to come." Marion tucked Rachel back under the covers. "But first, how about a bit more rest?"

What a week, thought Rachel. There were no words for how strange it all was.

L uke came into the room and sat in a chair near Rachel. "How are you, Chief?"

"I'm alive, Luke. That's more than anyone could have said a few hours ago. And I'm cancer-free, thanks to Marion. I have no idea how all that worked, but I'm grateful it did."

Luke's face contorted for a minute. "You were dead, Rachel. Your heart stopped. I saw your body."

"I know." She patted his hand. "We'll all be processing that night for a while."

Luke wiped his eyes. "Sorry. I know this is about you, not me. The main thing is for you to get your strength back."

"Yes. And do you know how I'm going to get my strength back?"

Luke shivered. "I have some idea."

"Marion has explained it to me. From now on, all my sustenance must come from blood. For the time being, it will be expired or contaminated blood."

"What about living people's blood? Are you going to suck my blood? Should I be scared of you?"

Rachel turned to Marion. "Should he?"

"No. Luke, these questions you've had about our blood bank are all answered by one simple fact: We exist for the ethical feeding of vampires. And we serve mortal patients too. But our whole system is devoted to providing food to our kind without harming anyone."

"Our. Who do you mean when you say "our?""

"The night shift, for one thing."

"You mean Sybil?"

"Vampire."

"And everyone who works here at night?"

"Vampires."

He shook his head. "Then it's really true. They're all vampires."

"Yes. The day shift serves mortal patients. The night shift serves immortal appetites."

"And that's why you have extra labels and extra blood bags?"

"Yes."

"And why you have conservative expiration dates?"

"Yes."

"Because you're—" The wheels were spinning in Luke's head. "You're labeling something that looks like blood as expired blood and sending it to be destroyed."

"That's right."

"But it's really water mixed with red food coloring and cornstarch."

"Exactly."

"And you set aside the real blood, which is still okay to feed your kind."

"That's true."

"And the same for blood that is infected with pathogens?"

Marion nodded.

"Because our diseases cannot make you sick."

"True. Except cancer." Marion smiled a wan smile. "I struggled for a minute with that one."

"And you know,—" said Rachel, "—they're also developing artificial blood that will help humans and also feed vampires." Rachel laughed. "All those suspicions we had about these people, and they're actually doing something good."

"Yes. And something totally illegal."

"Lots of things have been illegal over time, Luke. Teaching slaves to read. Lending money to women. Voting if you didn't own property. Hiding Jews from the Gestapo. Maybe the ethical feeding of the living dead will change too."

"Are you saying FDA should write regulations for blood intended for vampires?"

Rachel smiled. "Maybe someday. For now, I'm thankful this place exists."

Luke stood up. "Get some rest now, Rachel." He looked around. "I'm going to go have breakfast. I don't think I'm up for being here when you feed. No offense."

"None taken."

Luke looked back at Rachel. "And before I go, what are we going to write in our report?"

Rachel smiled. "There is no 'we.' I'm officially dead, Luke. It's your report now. What do you want it to say?"

Luke shook his head. "Wow. If I tell the truth…"

"Hundreds of hungry vampires will be unleashed on the state of Illinois."

"But if I lie…"

"You go against everything you've sworn to do."

He turned to Marion. "What about Amber?"

"What about her?"

"Now that we're telling the whole truth, is she… one of your kind? She says not. But I have to know for sure."

"Amber is an ally," said Marion. "A mortal ally. She is tremendously helpful. Essential, really. I will soon age out of this location because my kind don't visibly age, so we can't stay anywhere long enough to rouse suspicion. And when that day comes, Amber will take my place. That's assuming she isn't in jail as a result of your report."

Rachel sat up in bed. "Luke, I was an FDA inspector for decades. I took my job seriously and never misrepresented the facts. And I can't ask you to do any differently. Yet if you think about our true purpose at FDA, to protect public health, well, that might lead you in a different direction than you ever expected to go."

Amber came into the room then and took Luke's hand. "I'm glad Rachel is here with us."

"Me too. I thought she was going to die."

"She did."

"You know what I mean."

"Yes. And I know all this is extra hard for you because of your job."

"Yep."

"It was hard for me too when I first found out. I was hired to help run this blood bank and had no idea what was really going on. But it was not long before I began to realize what else they were doing. Marion kept dropping hints and eventually I got it."

"And what happened then?"

"Then I had a moment like you are having now."

"And you're still here."

"Yes. Marion is an amazing manager and she's doing so much good for people like us and for her people too. And until now she's been able to keep a lid on the whole thing."

"You mean she's been able to fool the inspectors."

Amber nodded. "Yes. You and Rachel have been exceptional."

"And what good did it do us?"

"You found me. And Rachel? Her life was saved."

"True. Very true. Alright. I'm in. My report will be a boring read."

Amber kissed him. "You'll be glad you came on board."

"Maybe I already am."

AT HIGHLAND HOUSE
CHAPTER NINETEEN

It was all over now: the dissembling, the half-answered questions. All over except one thing. As they left Rachel's basement room, Luke took Amber's hand.

"Have you ever been to Highland House?"

"Not to stay there; is it nice?"

"It's OK. The room service is pretty good."

Amber smiled. "Is this an invitation?"

"Sure. Want to come by?"

"Rather forward for a first date."

"Uh-huh. That's me, a forward kind of guy."

~

They closed the door of his hotel room and stood just inside it, kissing. Amber took Luke's hand in hers and kissed his fingers, one by one. Then she licked them, licked in between his fingers, gave each one a small bite. He put his head back and enjoyed it, but when she started biting he said, "Hey! You told me you weren't a vampire."

"Just practicing. One day I'll graduate. Maybe you will too."

He laughed. "Graduate? Is that what you call it?"

"Sure." She undid his tie. "I've been wanting to do this since the day we met. Wanting to see what you're like without all this folderol."

"Is that what this is? Folderol? I thought it was a tie." He leaned against the inside of the door, enjoying her as she explored his body. She slid her hands down his arms, inside his suit jacket, and slid it off him and onto the floor.

"Shirt next?" He leaned down to kiss her.

"Don't distract me." She undid his buttons, untucked his shirt, and pulled it off one arm and then the other. He was suddenly chilled, there in his undershirt.

"Can we get in bed now?"

"In a bit of a hurry, aren't we?"

"Well, yes, and also I'm cold."

"Come on, then." She took his hand and pulled him to the bed, turned down the covers, got in.

"Hey, you're still dressed," he said with mock indignation.

"I took my shoes off."

"No, that's not enough. Not nearly enough." He managed to pull her dress over her head while kissing her, with a brief intermission. And there she was, in almost all her glory, in this bed where he had imagined her so often. Luke stopped to look at her.

"What's wrong?" She asked.

"Nothing. Nothing at all is wrong." He reached around and unhooked her brassiere, then suddenly pushed her over onto the mattress. She, laughing, tried to undo his belt buckle. "I can't reach with you lying on top of me."

"That's fine. Let's take our time."

"But hurry," she said.

Their legs entwined, they kissed. And then when she came up for air, Amber said, "What do you suppose Rachel and Marion are doing right now?"

"I don't know. Maybe this? Can a medieval vampire even do it?"

"Luke! That's really ageist."

"What? You don't think five hundred is too old for sex?"

She pushed him off and sat up. "Would you think that if Marion were a guy?"

He paused. How to answer that? "Well…"

"So you're sexist and ageist too? Tell you what: Why don't you ask them about their sex life tomorrow?"

"Oh no. I'm not tangling with Marion. That woman is too scary."

"And what about this woman? Hmm?"

"You, my dear, are just the right amount of scary."

"Why, thank you. I think."

"May we resume, then?" He ran his hands across her ample derriere. "I promise to find you sexy at every age."

"Even five hundred?"

"Of course. Absolutely gorgeous at five hundred."

"Then you may proceed, Inspector."

And he did.

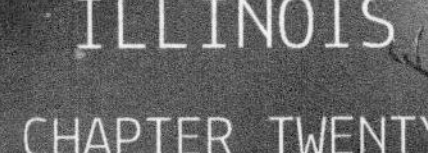

ILLINOIS
CHAPTER TWENTY

Marion walked into Rachel's room and was surprised to find her up and about. "What are you doing?"

"Getting dressed. I'm feeling much better today."

"And where are you going once you're dressed?"

"Out. After dark, I'm going out. Can't stay down here forever."

"Alright, if you insist. If you run into someone you know, you can always deny that you're you."

"Hmm. While wearing my own clothes?"

"Good point. I could order you something, if you don't want to wear your old clothes to go out shopping."

"How long will that take? A couple days, right?"

"Yes. But in the meantime you can wear something of mine. We're close to the same size." Marion handed her a tube of sunscreen from the dresser. "Here, put on some of this. It's almost twilight. We can go in a few minutes."

"Go where?"

"My place. I have a walk-in closet full of clothes I never wear."

"I thought you slept here."

"Usually. But sometimes I need a break."

They drove in Marion's Maserati and put the top down once the sun set. Marion's not-so-humble abode turned out to be a two-story Greek Revival mansion in elegant Lake Forest. The caretaker cottage in the back had once been Marion's laboratory, long ago when she lived there with Walter.

"Everybody in this neighborhood has multiple homes, so the fact that I'm not around much doesn't rouse suspicion. It works out."

"Yes, I suppose it would. But if you don't mind my asking, how do you…"

"Afford all this? I inherited the house from a mortal spouse. And, you know, I've had patents. And then there's investment income over hundreds of years." Marion shrugged. "Typical vampire stuff."

"Hundreds of years," Rachel repeated. "You really do think of me as young, don't you?"

Marion parked the Maserati and turned to Rachel, smiling. "You have no idea. Those people you told me about in Zion, who refused to believe that the earth orbits the sun? Well, that was everybody when I was young."

"When was that?"

"The mid-1500s, in England. Copernicus knew the truth, but almost no one else did."

"The sixteenth century?"

"Yes. When I was mortal, the horse-drawn carriage was high tech. Medical care was mostly bloodletting. I was an herbal healer and did some good, I think. And was tried as a witch for my trouble."

Rachel shook her head. "Incredible. It will take me a while to understand all this."

"I have a hard time grasping it myself, and I've had ages to adjust. With so many memories, I end up not thinking about whole centuries for years at a time. Even the brain of a vampire has only so much space." Marion smiled. "Best to live in the moment. Come on, let's go get you some clothes."

The inside of the house was as elegant as the outside. A two-story circular foyer featured a winding staircase. To her left Rachel could see a spacious living room with an oversized fireplace, and to her right was a formal dining room with a crystal and chrome light fixture. Marion barely paused. "These rooms don't get much use. When I'm here, I'm mainly in the basement. I had it redone after I inherited it. Come, let me show you."

The word "basement" did not do justice to the downstairs floor where Marion led Rachel. The walls were a warm peach with pale cream trim, and above the high ceiling a crystal chandelier reflected rainbows. Off the main room was the master suite (or "Mistress Suite," as the lady of the house called it). And Marion's closet was exactly as advertised: huge and filled with clothes that still bore their tags. Rachel tried to ignore the prices, which were way outside her paygrade. Former paygrade, she reminded herself.

Rachel emerged in a black designer suit with a cinnamon shell underneath. She had dressed carefully, with dark hose, black wedge heel shoes, and gold jewelry with a classic appeal. She walked out to the bedroom and stood in front of Marion. "How do I look?"

She looked healthy. She looked happy. She looked bright and alert. To Marion, she looked just like Cecily would have looked, if Cecily had lived into her fifties, and if Cecily had the chance to develop as Rachel had done. Rachel looked, in a word, irresistible.

After Marion took Rachel in her arms, shoes, hose, suit jacket, pencil skirt, all were cast aside. Hands were everywhere: caressing breasts, touching shoulders, massaging buttocks. Rachel's hands slid behind Marion's head and pulled her close. She found Marion's lips with her own, lips that tasted of time, the spices of long ago, the herbs in the garden of her burnt English cottage. Rachel could sense the remnants of iron on Marion's tongue, the errant proteins of expired blood. The taste thrilled her as if the blood were Marion's own.

Marion slid her hand between Rachel's legs and her hand was cool as stone, cool as a spring breeze across the Yorkshire hills. Marion breathed softly into Rachel's ear as her hand slid up the sensitive skin at the inside of Rachel's thigh.

Rachel thrilled at the heightened sense of touch she experienced in Marion's arms. "Kiss me again. Please. Give me your tongue." With a low murmur, Marion did as she was asked.

Still kissing, the two made their way to Marion's bed, which was large and inviting, a slightly darker peach than the walls, with a generous silken canopy. Lying on it, Rachel felt as if she were floating in space. Marion's body was strong and soft, new and somehow familiar. Her fingers teased Rachel's nipples while her lips kissed Rachel's neck and gave her the tiniest of bites, a reminder of their exchange of blood just two days before. Rachel could not consciously remember that moment, yet some part of her thrilled at the reminder. She wanted to touch Marion too, but the sensations Marion gave her were so overwhelming that all she could do was moan through her kisses.

For Marion, stroking Rachel's body brought back memories of lying in a spring meadow with Cecily. Rachel's skin, the sounds Rachel made in desire, the way she held her limbs when excited, her wide-eyed gaze, all echoed that ecstatic time, and yet Rachel was new and fresh and in this present moment.

Later, as she lay in Marion's arms and played with a lock of her hair, Rachel said, "I thought we were going to wait a while."

Marion smiled. "I did too. After all, we have plenty of time. Then suddenly I was finished waiting. How about you?"

Rachel kissed her cheek. "Yes, I was ready, and I'm glad you were too."

Marion turned out the light, but with their heightened senses, they could clearly see one another's bodies—their lovely immortal bodies. And in Rachel's case, the body that was supposed to be in a sealed coffin at the funeral home, awaiting burial. But no truly dead body ever experienced what Rachel felt that night in Marion's arms.

CHAPTER TWENTY-ONE

Rachel's son Victor was long, thin and anxious looking. And although he did not know it, he could have passed for the older brother of Rachel's mentee, Luke. But Victor was no scientist. He was an economist who taught about cryptocurrency in London and was celebrating the end of the semester. All that was left was finals week, after which a bigger celebration was in order.

Dinner out with his girlfriend Claudia was interrupted by news of his mother's death.

Victor looked at the text on his phone and put down his wine glass. "What is it?" asked Claudia.

"It's my mother. She's died."

"Oh, Vic, I'm so sorry."

"The funeral is next week. Finals week. There is no way I can leave school during finals week for a funeral."

"Of course you can go, Vic," said Claudia.

Liam shook his head. "I really can't, Claudia. I'm on thin ice at school as it is."

"Why?"

"They just don't like me. I've never understood why. Maybe it's my subject matter. Too edgy for the London School of Economics."

"Well, I like you."

"Yes, I know."

She took his hand across the table. "I'm sorry about your mother."

"Thank you." He shook his head. "How strange. I didn't even know she was ill."

Rachel's daughter Olivia looked a lot like her mother. She was somewhat severe, with a prominent jaw and close-cropped hair. Olivia was a tour guide at the Tower of London, was great at shepherding big crowds without letting anyone fall behind. She was on the bus home when her cell phone rang, from a U.S. number she did not recognize.

Sorry to tell you… sorry for your loss… peaceably early this morning…

The bus was so noisy she could not really hear. Who could it be? Someone had died, someone had called. She hung up the phone unsure what it all meant.

It was not until the next day when the funeral home called that Olivia found out her mother had died.

Oh no, she thought. *Mother is so healthy.* Was it a prank? No, it was real alright. And there was no way she could afford to fly home.

And then she thought about half the proceeds of her mother's house coming to her, but too late for the funeral. And then she felt guilty, and only then did she cry.

Luke walked into the FDA Chicago District Office a few days before Rachel's funeral to present his inspection report on the Lake County Blood Bank. The findings were unremarkable: six minor deviations. Luke estimated that the few problems cited would be corrected within a month. He was glad to put the whole thing behind him before the funeral. The report he filed was not wrong, he reassured himself; it was simply incomplete.

His colleagues commiserated with him on the loss of the Chief. He had a hard time knowing what to say, especially when one of them said, "She's still with us in spirit."

Especially after dark was the first thing that came to mind, but he managed to contain himself.

When the day arrived for Rachel's service, the chapel was packed with serious-looking FDA staff in a range of suit colors from black to navy, plus a few outliers in charcoal gray. Luke sat near the front with two other inspectors who had reported directly to Rachel. At the front near the chancel was a mahogany coffin decorated with lilies and roses. He wondered what was really in there. *And to think that in the old days vampires actually slept in those things.* He shivered.

Rachel's children had not made it over from Europe; the bouquets they had sent stood at either side of the coffin. Those poor kids were not even aware that their mother was (more or less) alive. He looked down at the Order of Service to hide his emotion.

Luke went through the motions during the funeral, singing when it was time to sing, listening politely to the speeches. Because Rachel had left a will but no instructions for her service, her mother Jenny had chosen the minister: a fundamentalist whose sermon was full of claims that the dead shall rise again. Rachel would have found that hilarious had she snuck into the chapel. At least Jenny was comforted by her religion. It was probably more comfort to her, Luke thought, than if she knew the truth.

It was surreal to think the whole thing was really a retirement party, minus the guest of honor. Luke planned to skip the reception. He had to show up for the service, of course, sham that it was. Not to do so would have been suspicious. But the thought of talking with his colleagues about his supposedly deceased superior was just too weird. He could not pretend that she was dead. At least, not yet.

The service ended, finally. He scoped out the nearest exit and was on his way when he heard his name.

"Luke!" It was Rachel's manager, Todd Sterling. "Hey, walk with me to the reception and have a glass of wine. I know we don't drink during work hours, but today is different."

Luke could hardly say no.

Luke looked around at his colleagues, clustered in little groups, speaking softly and respectfully as they chugged down the wine. Todd took his elbow.

"Listen, Luke, first wanted to say how sorry I am about Rachel. I know she was a mentor to you, and she was your friend too, eh?"

Luke nodded, looking down at the glass of chardonnay Todd pressed into his hand.

"And I also want to say the report you filed on LCBB was first rate. Really. I paid special attention because I knew it was the first writeup where you were in charge. Looking forward to more from you." Todd clapped him on the shoulder. "Must say you and Rachel did a bang-up job on that inspection, and you captured the findings clearly. Is Lake County addressing its violations?"

"Yes. They've started sending corrective actions. I've scheduled a follow-up inspection for next month."

"Good. Very good." Todd lowered his voice, dipped his head closer to Luke's. "Just one thing: Was there any way Rachel's death could have been linked to that blood bank? Crazy question, I know. It's just I've never had an inspector die while onsite. I want to be sure there's nothing we've overlooked."

Luke looked Todd in the eye. "I can definitely tell you there was nothing going on at that blood bank that could have damaged Rachel's health. The cancer in her brain caused a stroke. That's all."

Todd shook Luke's hand. "That's what I wanted to hear. Thanks Luke. Again, sorry for your loss."

The night following her funeral, Rachel was quite busy for someone who was supposed to be in the ground. On the cusp of her new role as night-shift manager at the blood bank, she stood with Marion at the top of the basement stairs.

She was just a tiny bit nervous. "I feel like Mark Twain: Reports of my death have been greatly exaggerated."

Marion laughed at that. "I get it. And so will your new direct reports."

Rachel squeezed Marion's hand. "Thank you. Thank you for saving me, and thank you for giving me a purpose in this new life."

"You're so welcome," said Marion. "Come on. They're dying to meet you."

"You had to say that, didn't you?"

"Yes, I did."

Rachel made her way down the stairs and shook hands with the former Sisters of Camden House, now medical technicians in white lab coats. Sybil and Gwen she almost recognized, somehow. The rest were new to her. Thankfully they all wore nametags.

"Greetings, everyone," said Marion, calling the staff to attention. Rachel noticed how much more relaxed Marion was with these women than she had been during the inspection. Marion continued, "I'd like to introduce the newest member of our staff. Some of you may remember Dr. Rachel Sutter as our latest FDA inspector, and a thorough inspector she was. But Rachel has switched teams, which is FDA's loss and our gain. She joins us as manager of the night shift and will be involved with everything we do on this floor: Both the research for an acceptable artificial blood, and serving our evening customers. Please give Rachel Sutter a hand."

Applause and smiles greeted Rachel. Sarah Clarke walked up to her and shook her hand.

"Welcome to the night shift," said Sarah. "We're very glad to have you. Your expertise will be so helpful. And how great that you've come over to the dark side." Indeed, it was dark outside, though in a windowless basement, who could tell.

"Thank you," said Rachel, "and thanks to all of you for making me feel right at home. I look forward to learning more about your research, and how you serve your nocturnal clientele."

"What's the first thing you're going to do as manager?" asked Sybil.

"Learn all of your names," said Rachel, to polite laughter. "And then review your procedures—because I am ex-FDA, after all. Then I'll dig into your research. It's been a long time since I was in a research lab, so please bear with me."

"It's like riding a bicycle," said Marion. "You'll do just fine."

And as it turned out, she did.

Years later when he looked back, Luke was not sure how he got through Rachel's funeral. But he did know how important that day was to his future. From there, Luke moved up in the FDA hierarchy, and he always credited what he had learned from Rachel. Of course no one knew what he meant: That she was immortal because of diverted blood, and still gave him advice whenever he asked.

And as years went by, no one was suspicious when Luke developed a speciality in inspecting every blood bank East of the Rockies that shared one thing in common: They all had night shifts.

NEXT MOVES

CHAPTER TWENTY-TWO

It was morning in Marion's Lake Forest basement, though there were no windows to prove it. Rachel lay her head on Marion's chest. Marion stirred.

"Don't move, Marion. Not yet."

"What are you doing?"

"Listening to your heartbeat. Your very slow heartbeat."

"What about it?"

"I'm just thinking. How can you be dead if your heart is beating?"

Marion smiled. "The first question Amber asked when she learned about vampires was 'How does your immune system work if you're dead?'"

Rachel sat up. "Exactly! Do you know?"

"No idea. As I told her, I've been busy these past five hundred years trying to stay alive. And finding a way for us to see daylight without vaporizing. And making sure we have ways to eat that don't involve murdering people."

"Of course. You've been doing applied research."

Marion laughed and propped herself on one elbow. "You could call it that."

Rachel nodded. "There's nothing wrong with applied science. But what about basic science? Don't you want to know the answers to all the questions, like: Why do we live so long? Why does sunlight kill us? Why don't we catch human diseases? Why can we see beyond the usual human wavelengths? And since you're into applied science, just imagine the applications of those answers, for vampire health and for human health."

"Oh no. Wait a minute." Marion sat up, cross-legged, on the bed. "If you think we have a population problem today, what would it be like if everybody lived eight hundred years?"

"That's fair."

"And do you really want vampires without scruples, and believe me, they're out there, free to wander around in broad daylight?"

"I get it. You're not wrong."

"So what exactly *do* you want?"

"I want to understand us. All about us. Are we dead, or just different? Are we infected with some organism that makes us the way we are? And if that's true, what kind of bug is it? How about you, Marion, aren't you curious?"

Marion put her hand on Rachel's knee. "You're a real scientist, aren't you? Not a tinkerer like me. So what do you want to do next, Doctor Curious? After all, zero research dollars are devoted to exploring vampire anatomy and physiology."

"We could change that. Carefully. I'm sure you're not the only rich vampire."

"OK. We can talk about the whole funding piece. And I admit that over the centuries, as the human body became better understood, I've resented that I know so little about the function of my own body. I could read a thousand studies about the mortal immune system, for example, but I'd never learn why it is that I, a dead woman, do not simply rot away."

"Precisely."

"I know what it feels like to become a vampire, and now so do you. And I know what a rush it is to create another vampire. But what is that process, biochemically? Sure, I'm a scientist. I haven't always looked like one, or been accepted as one, but I've always been one—

even back in my stone cottage days. And yet life is so busy. When would I have had time to investigate all this?"

Rachel shook her head. "Is time really the issue? Or are you afraid of what you will find? I mean, when I was a kid, I snuck a book of Ray Bradbury stories into the house. Had to sneak; all science fiction was totally evil, according to my mother. Bradbury grew up in Waukegan, you know. He wrote an entire story collection that took place in small-town Illinois. There was this one story about a boy whose mother runs a boarding house, and the boy discovers one of his mom's boarders is a vampire. The boy cuts open the vampire in the middle of the day, while it is asleep and helpless. Turns out its organs are geometrical: spongy purple triangles, soft blue squares. I used to dream about that story at night, that I was palpating my own organs, discovering my heart is a rectangle and my intestines a double spiral."

Marion reached for Rachel. "So… let me palpate your organs… nope, no triangles here."

Rachel laughed and tried to fend her off. "Stop it! That tickles! Seriously now: Have you ever sequenced your genome?"

"No."

"Have you even looked at your cells under a microscope?"

"No."

"Why not?"

"I'm afraid they might look like little tiny Satan faces."

Rachel laughed. "You can take the girl out of the Middle Age…"

"Hey. I'm not middle aged. Five hundred is genuinely old."

"Good one. Marion, this is our moment to do something new. Amber is ready to take over the blood bank. Luke will keep the FDA out of her hair. And you've been here too many years without changing."

"I could dye my hair white."

"You could. Or purple. And as for me, I need to get out of Chicagoland before somebody sees me and figures out I'm not dead. Why don't we start a research lab somewhere? Somewhere far away? Will you think it over?"

"Sure." Marion shrugged. "I haven't thought about much lately, except surviving your inspection."

Rachel kissed Marion and snuggled up to her. "Here, I promise you'll survive—let me inspect you."

"That wasn't on my schedule."

"All my inspections are unannounced."

THE RETURN OF VIVIENNE
CHAPTER TWENTY-THREE

Vivienne had been absent from Marion's life for going on half a millennium when she made her way to Highland Park. It was a stormy Friday in April when Vivienne, still the strongest vampire Marion had ever known, arrived at the Lake County Blood Bank.

When the receptionist called to say she had a visitor, Marion walked out to the lobby and saw a woman she had never expected to encounter again. After centuries on earth, very little surprised Marion enough to leave her speechless. But in that moment, she stood without a word and stared at her old friend.

"Well, Marion. Have you nothing to say?"

Marion clasped the other woman's hand. "Vivienne. You're alive! I've looked for you and found no trace."

"I don't want to leave a trace. In fact, I work hard to be untraceable. It gets harder all the time."

In the last five hundred years, Vivienne had continued her work rescuing mortal women from danger. She had travelled the world, looking for ways to make a difference and finding plenty of them, mostly in remote places. But now she was stepping back into the life of cities and industrialized nations. Now she was seeking support in her mission. And stepping back meant looking for Marion, whom she had never forgotten.

Vivienne gestured at their surroundings. "A remarkable career you're having, my friend."

"Thank you. I'm sure I could say the same about you if I knew what you were doing." Marion led her friend to her office.

Vivienne smiled. "We get around. It's amazing what you learn about people, and power, in six hundred years."

Marion nodded. "And the money you make."

"Yes, that too. Didn't you inherit a good bit, somewhere along the way?"

"I did. And earned some. It's great how interest accrues over the centuries."

"Indeed," said Vivienne. "We estimate five percent of the world's wealth is now held by vampires. And counting. And over half of that by female vampires."

"Really? The gender split on wealth is way different for mortals."

"Female vampires live longer, by centuries, than the men. It's not about our natural lifespans. Men just keep doing stupid shit, even when they're dead." Vivienne looked at the test equipment visible through the office window. "And I suppose you know what all this stuff does?"

"I do."

"You always were a healer."

"These days the whole world needs healing."

"Yes. That's what I'm here to see you about." Vivienne came back to stand in front of Marion. "Remember way back in York when you asked to join us?"

"Yes, I remember very well. You turned me down."

"Because you were too new. Back then you barely knew how to make another vampire. Frankly I wasn't sure how you would turn out."

Marion suppressed a smile. "And how did I?"

Vivienne smiled, a rarity for her. "King Henry's men turned up at Camden House while you lot were asleep at the Twelve Apostles.

Trashed the place. Good on you for getting everyone out safely. Not to mention everything you've done since. A witch turned nurse turned inventor turned tech business owner? I'd say you've done pretty well."

"So what's your offer?"

"You're right about the world. The whole place needs healing. And I'm sensing that you are ready to make a move."

Marion gestured at her surroundings. "I've run this blood bank for fifteen years. I look exactly the same as the day I started."

"Yes." Vivienne nodded. "There's nothing like being undead to teach Buddhist non-attachment. But I sense you're attached to the people here."

"One always is."

"And speaking of attachments, you just created a new vampire."

"Rachel? Yes. She needs a new persona more urgently than I do. She died very publicly. She can't go on with her old gig for one more day, much less one more year. And by the way, wherever I go needs to welcome her too."

Vivienne raised an eyebrow. "So you two are partners?"

"We are. We have shared more than blood."

"Too bad. I was kind of hoping, now that you and I are more or less peers..."

Marion shrugged. "Your timing is off, Vivienne. There were centuries when I would have welcomed you as a lover."

"Ah well. Death is long. In the meantime, tell me about her. What's she made of? Is she tough enough to be an operative?"

"She was tougher than me even when she was mortal. I have never seen such problem solving, such tenacity. She is formidable now."

Vivienne nodded. "If you vouch for her, that is enough."

"So, where are you off to next?"

"How is your Russian?"

"Pretty good, actually. I spent some time in Moscow when they were doing early transfusion work. Why?"

"Get your friend Rachel to take a crash course in Russian, then let's meet in Paris in six months."

"So you're taking on whole governments now?"

Vivienne nodded. "Killing assholes like Anna Marshall's husband is all well and good. But if we are really in the business of saving women's lives, we have to think big. And here in the United States too, for that matter." Another rare smile from Vivienne. "Just think what one of us could do with a lifetime judicial appointment."

"I'll check in with Rachel, see what she wants to do. But I must tell you, we're in the process of making a different plan. Rachel wants to create an institute to study vampire physiology and metabolism. She's convinced that what we find out could have lots of applications, for us and for mortals. But mostly she just wants to learn what makes us tick."

Vivienne nodded. "I can see that being a great next move for you. This biology stuff is not my cup of tea, but it's important. Do you have enough seed money?"

"Not quite."

"You might talk with Kate, from your old Sisterhood."

"Kate! She's the only one of the Sisters I've never found."

"I'm not surprised. Kate is especially discrete, almost like me. She's a major philanthropist in England, with a particular interest in the sciences. I'll put you in touch."

"Thanks. The other Sisters will be glad to hear that Kate is alright."

"And where are the others?"

Marion smiled. "They're all here, on night staff at the blood bank, developing artificial blood."

"Every one of them?"

"Yes, aside from Kate. Would you like to say hello?"

"I would! And I might try to steal one or two of them away for my project, if you don't mind. There are some badass women in that crew."

"Their shift starts at six. Come back then and I'll take you downstairs." Marion reached out and they shook hands. "Best of luck, Vivienne."

"And to you, and Rachel. It's all for the good of the planet. And we undead are the ones who can pull it off."

Marion walked downstairs to the artificial blood lab and found Rachel. "My old friend Vivienne is coming by later. She wants to see the Sisters after all these years, and she wants to meet you too."

Rachel looked up from her computer. "Terrific! She's the woman who saved you, right?"

"Yes. And something she said reminded me: I never asked where in Europe your kids are, exactly."

"Victor teaches at the London School of Economics. And Olivia is a tour guide at the Tower."

"Both in London."

"Yes."

"You want to move to England."

"I'd love that! And I'll bet you have thought about going back."

Marion smiled. "I'm certainly thinking about it now."

RACHEL'S ANNIVERSARY
CHAPTER TWENTY-FOUR

It had been exactly one year since Rachel had died and been reborn as a vampire. To celebrate, Marion, Rachel, Amber and Luke stood in the dining room of Amber's condo, each with a wineglass in hand, though none of the glasses contained wine. Amber and Luke had sparkling cider, and Luke stared at the clear liquid in Marion and Rachel's wineglasses, wondering what it was.

"Here's to Rachel," said Luke, and they all lifted their glasses. "Happy Vampire Anniversary, to the best boss who ever came back to life—but not to work."

"Here's to my darling love," said Marion, putting her arm around Rachel's shoulder. "I am so grateful we found each other." They kissed, an embarrassingly long kiss.

"Thank you all," said Rachel. "It's been quite the year. Now, let's drink, before our arms get tired."

"Um, not to be nosy but—what is that clear stuff in your glasses?" asked Luke.

"Expired plasma," said Rachel. She shrugged. "Not at all interesting, but we can drink it."

Marion wrinkled her nose. "But it doesn't taste like much."

"You don't really have to drink it," said Rachel. "It's just for effect."

"Well, this cake isn't just for effect, at least not for me," said Luke, cutting himself a piece.

"I'll have some too, Babe," said Amber, reaching past her pregnant belly to take a slice. Her wedding with Luke had been at night, so that Marion and Rachel could sit holding hands in the back mezzanine of the church and observe, even though Rachel was officially dead.

After Rachel's apparent demise, Luke had taken on the senior role in inspections. And Amber was taking on more and more of a leadership role at the Lake County Blood Bank. Even though Marion now dyed her hair completely grey, she was becoming uneasy about staying in one place so long.

"We have an announcement," said Marion. "Rachel and I have decided it's time to make our move. With Rachel's children both working in Europe, we are going to relocate with new names and identities to a place overseas where we can start over, no questions asked."

"I'm always wondering when somebody I know from FDA will wander into the night shift at the blood bank," Rachel said. "And frankly, I'm sick of hiding out in the basement. It's a bit claustrophobic down there."

"And I'm always wondering when somebody is going to compare my photo ten years ago with how I look now and decide I keep a painting of myself in my nonexistent attic. And this way, I get to visit my old stomping grounds in Northern England."

"Wow." Amber set down her glass. "I'm not sure that I'm ready for this. Especially with the baby coming."

"You'll be terrific, Amber." Rachel patted her shoulder. "And you'll never have to worry about sleeping through the night. The whole night shift will volunteer."

Luke shivered at the thought of a team of vampires caring for his firstborn. But he got over it quickly. After all, those vampires were pledged to take no blood from living humans. That was why the Lake

County Blood Bank was essential. What did Marion always say? "We will take no blood before its time."

"We'll miss you," Luke said. "Both of you. But we understand it's what you need to do. But how will you let your children know you're alive without giving them a heart attack?"

"We have a plan," said Rachel.

Amber asked, "And what will you do when you get there? Start another blood bank?"

Marion shook her head. "No. We are setting up an institute where we'll do basic research on vampire biochemistry."

Rachel's face lit up. "It's a whole new field! You know how people rightly complain there's not enough medical research on women after menopause? Well, it's even worse for women vampires. As in, zero dollars."

Sarah organized a baby shower for Amber that was straight out of *The Addams Family*. Black streamers hung from the walls of the downstairs lab, and the conference room table held white cupcakes with little sugar skulls on top. There were two bowls of punch: one was blood-red, and the other was actual blood. Amber arrived while Sarah was just setting out black cups and napkins.

"I love it!" Amber was ecstatic. "Did you know I was a Goth in high school?"

"Really? That's fantastic. I had no idea," said Sarah. "But you'll have to ditch the nipple piercings to feed the baby."

Amber laughed. "I got rid of those a while ago. Luke was not a fan."

The staff arrived at the appointed hour, bearing gifts. Rachel hugged Amber and handed her a small present. "Here, Amber. Open this first."

Amber opened the box and lifted out a small black cross on a beaded chain. "It's beautiful. Just the kind of thing I used to wear in my Goth phase."

Rachel smiled. "It *is* a bit Goth, isn't it? And might seem an odd present from a little old atheist like me. But really, it's from all of us downstairs folk."

Amber looked closely at her gift. "How odd. There's a button in the middle. Not your standard cross, then."

"No, except one thing: Remember in the old movies when people used crosses to ward off vampires? We wanted you to have some extra protection while you're pregnant in case you run into trouble with our downstairs clientele. Most of the undead are well-behaved, but you never know. Just press that button if you need us."

Amber looked around at the women in the room, vampires every one, and some of the best people she had ever known. "Thank you all. I'm honored. And I will wear this every day."

Two weeks later, Marion handed her office key to Amber and looked around the building one last time. Night was falling. As she said goodbye, Marion could sense that the Lake County Blood Bank was haunted: Not just by the night shift who were all, like her, children of the night, but also by the souls of those they had saved. And they had saved not only the patients who received blood but also the humans who had not become prey to Marion's own kind.

A month later, on a moonlit night, Marion sat at the bar at The Green Man pub in York. The last time she had sat in that room and pretended to drink ale was during the reign of Henry VIII. Despite the electric lighting and the telly on the wall with an Australian cricket match showing, the place looked remarkably the same, with its dark wood pilasters, its beamed ceiling, and its long oak tables. Marion chatted with the bartender, who turned out to be the owner—and a descendent of the man who had owned the place back in her time.

Back in my time. Isn't this my time too? Marion was never sure.

When the clock struck eight, she moved from the bar to an ancient dark wood table to wait for two very special guests.

Olivia and her brother Victor walked in at the appointed hour. Marion recognized them both from pictures Rachel had shown her—and in Olivia's case, by her resemblance to Rachel, and to Cecily. Marion waved them over.

Marion had never had children, never wanted children, yet the sight of these two young people moved her. But Olivia and Victor did not return the smile she gave them as she offered them seats at the table.

"How was the train from London?" asked Marion.

"Fine. It was fine. You said you had information about our mother," said Olivia, sitting with her arms crossed.

"We felt terrible that we were not able to come to her memorial," said Victor.

"I'm sure she would understand," said Marion. "Such a caring person, your mother."

"How did you know her?"

"Your mother and I had—have a very special bond," said Marion. "I know no one could take the place of your other mom, whose loss you must feel terribly. But I hope you'll come to see me as, perhaps, a helpful aunt."

Olivia and Victor looked at each other. "That's kind of you, but we don't know you. And we are orphans now." Olivia's voice caught a little. "We've lost both our mothers."

"I understand." Marion looked around the pub. "It's been a long time since I was here," she said. "The last time I sat in this room, I heard news that changed my life. And now, in a different way, your lives are about to change. And it won't be easy to understand, but trust me, under the circumstances it's the best news you could possibly have."

Victor frowned. "What? What's this about?"

Marion said nothing but nodded and pointed behind them.

They turned to see their mother Rachel, smiling at them, walking in the door.

RETURN OF THE ROCK STAR

CHAPTER TWENTY-FIVE

It was a long day. And being October, it was almost dark in the parking lot by the time Amber left the blood bank. Everyone said the second trimester was the easy part, but Amber was always tired now. All she wanted was to climb into her car, go home to Luke, and put her feet up. But someone was leaning on the hood of her car—someone who looked familiar.

"Hello Amber."

"Greg. Didn't expect to see you here."

He smiled; not, she thought, a very nice smile. "No, I bet you didn't. That's kind of the point. Thought I'd see how you were doing, now that your precious Marion is gone to England—poof!" He wiggled his fingers in the air.

Gregory walked up to Amber and put his hands on her belly. "And —oh my—looks like a two-for-one deal here. I've never tasted a pregnant woman before. Eating for two means bleeding for two, doesn't it, Baby? Or should I say Babies?"

"I've told you. I don't want to be a vampire."

"Oh, that ship has sailed. You're not going to be immortal. You're going to be my dinner." He pulled her closer, leaned in toward her neck, then stopped. "How quaint: a crucifix around your pretty neck. Do you really think they work?"

"This one does." Amber held up the black cross around her neck and pushed a button at its center.

"Should I cringe? Do a Bella Lugosi impression?" He looked up. "Oh, but we seem to be surrounded by ghosts."

Around them in the twilight, ten women in white coats assembled in a circle.

"The night shift." Gregory turned in a circle, facing the women. "Greetings, ladies. I understand you've foresworn the blood of live humans. So let me show you how it's done." He turned back to Amber, bared his impressive white teeth, and lurched forward.

Sybil stepped out of the circle and grabbed his arm. "Long before you were born, we swore to protect women from men like you."

"I am not just some man. I am immortal."

"Even immortals must die," said Gwen. The women surrounded Gregory, held him immobile.

Sarah turned to Amber. "It's best if you leave. A woman who is with child should not see this."

Amber nodded, got into her car and drove away from the sights and smells of what happened next. She stopped herself from glancing at her rear view mirror. The screams, though, followed her through the parking lot.

YORKSHIRE, 2025 (AND 2125)

CHAPTER TWENTY-SIX

Rachel stared out the window of the Mini as Marion drove up a narrow Yorkshire lane. "So this is where it started."

Marion nodded, keeping her eyes on the road as she guided the car between two stone walls on either side. "Yes. Nearby is where I hid from the world when I lost Cecily."

"It all looks so old. Has it changed much?"

"It's very different. For starters, we are driving to Whixton in a car, not riding a horse. Or walking." As they crested a rise, Marion looked ahead and gasped.

"What is it?"

"You see this grassland ahead? That was all forest. Except for a few fields of sheep grazing near the village. And now… fields everywhere." Marion found a gateway to a field where she could pull off the narrow road and look around.

The entire valley was grazing land now, with low stone walls separating farmers' fields from each other. Sheep grazed, lambs leaped. The lush forest of Marion's youth was reduced to a single stand of trees. Yet the place was still beautiful. The low valley of grass was surrounded by steep hills, all green in the morning light. And the streams and waterfalls Marion remembered could be seen from farther away now that the forest was gone.

It was hard to sort out exactly where she was. But as they drove through the valley, Marion caught sight of her own stone cottage. It was no longer hidden by woods but instead was at the edge of a field, near a stone wall that now bordered the road. Marion parked. She and Rachel walked through a wooden gate in the stone fence and over to the cottage.

Grass grew where Marion's herb gardens had been. The burnt thatched roof of the cottage had long since been replaced with slate. But Marion knew this was her home, not only by location, but by the size and shape of the doors and windows, and her memory of the stone walls themselves. She felt the cornerstone with her hand.

"Five hundred years," she said.

"What's this?" Rachel traced three interlocking triangles carved in a stone by the door.

"The men must have carved that after they burned the place. It's a symbol, intended to mean the Father, Son, and Holy Ghost. It's supposed to keep away witches." Marion laughed and put her hand on the carving. "Too late, you fools, we're here."

"Maybe the triangles really mean Maiden, Mother, Crone."

"Maybe so." Marion traced the door frame where the wolf had once breathed. "No more wolves now. The one that visited me was almost the last. Sheep farmers killed them all, and the deer have taken over. So now there is talk of reintroducing wolves in the North of England. Who knows? Maybe someday a wolf will stand at this doorway again."

Marion took Rachel's hand and led her back toward their car. "There is one more place to visit while we are here."

They parked in the village. Its two-story stone houses, that had looked imposing to Marion's eyes as a young woman, looked tiny and quaint to her now. The parking lot was next to the market square where she had sold jams and jellies, back in her mortal life. "Come this way," she said, and led Rachel to the Norman church at the center of town, with its stone walls and tall spire.

Inside they found a few women weaving bouquets for an upcoming festival. Marion looked around at the simple interior.

One of the village women walked over to them. "Hello, I'm Betty. May I help you?"

"I remember—I thought this church would be more ornate inside."

Betty smiled. "It was, back in medieval times. When this parish church was Catholic, services were in Latin and most in the village could not read. So there were paintings on all the walls portraying the stories of the Bible for the townspeople. There were incense burners, ornate iron candelabras, and at the back of the church hung elaborate robes for the priests. Imagine all that!"

Marion nodded politely. She did not need to imagine it, nor the stained glass windows now replaced by plain glass.

"But when Henry VIII broke from Rome, everything ornate was called 'Popish,' and removed from parish churches. And so we have this simplicity. Elegant, isn't it?" Betty smiled.

Marion smiled back, but wondered who had benefitted from selling off the pride of the village for pennies. She would not have put it past Cecily's sister Joan and her widower. But she would never know. Aloud she said, "And do you still keep a record of births and deaths in the parish? May we see it?"

"Yes, the books are here." Betty walked with them to a room lined with ancient books. "Anyone in particular you'd like to trace?"

"Thank you, yes. I'd like to trace the descendants of Grace Draper, born around 1545. She was the daughter of Cecily Draper."

"Here is the volume that includes 1545." Betty pulled an ancient book from the shelf. "These records show marriages, births and deaths. Feel free to peruse the books—carefully, of course. We are here all afternoon. I leave you to it."

"Thank you." Marion scanned the pages of the volume and found Grace's birth, and then her marriage, and finally her death in 1628. "Ah, baby girl," Marion whispered. "A good long life, especially for those times."

With Rachel's help, Marion found Grace's daughter and traced her life, and her daughter's life, all the way through the generations to Grace Ann Hebroth, born 1898.

"Look," said Marion, "This is where the trail ends. I don't see any marriage listed for this Grace, nor any death date."

"Grace Ann Hebroth." Rachel placed her hand on the page that recorded her birth, then turned to Marion, wide-eyed.

"What is it?"

"Grace Ann Hebroth was the maiden name of my great-grandmother. She left England for America as a young woman, married my great-grandfather and moved to Chicago."

Marion took Rachel's hands in hers. "So you are descended from Cecily."

"Yes, it seems that I am."

When they left the records room, Marion found their guide. "Thank you so much for everything. We're off now to visit Cecily Draper's grave."

"You're most welcome," said Betty. "And may I show you where she is buried? The markers from that era have long since crumbled."

"No, thank, you, we will be fine. I've visited Cecily's grave before."

Marion led Rachel to Cecily's burial plot. They stood together as clouds gathered and a fine mist began to fall. "Together, then apart, then together again," said Marion.

"What Mother Shipton said to you."

"And to you, Rachel."

As they left the churchyard, Rachel gave Marion's hand a squeeze. "So, what happens now? Will we live happily ever after?"

"That sounds lovely. Of course, there is no such thing as 'ever after.' Even immortals die someday. No census, but the mean lifespan of a vampire is around eight hundred years."

Rachel laughed. "You're so literal."

"I've been told that. But despite our eventual mortality, for beings like us, 'ever after' is a very long time."

"True."

"So, my love, how about we take it a century at a time?"

Rachel smiled. "It's a deal."
They walked hand in hand out the gate of the churchyard.

And a century later, after many more adventures, Marion and Rachel still walked hand in hand.

STELLA WOULD LOVE TO KNOW YOU BETTER!

Stella writes a regular blog and newsletter. A blog comes out—either from her or from a guest blogger[1]—on the 10th and 20th of the month. That's always related to being a woman past mid-life or the craft of writing [you can find Stella's manifesto here: https://stellafosse.com/stella-fosse-author/]. Stella's newsletter publishes at the end of each month.

You can sign up for Stella's Newsletter & Blog here: http://page.stellafosse.com/whats-new.

---

1. Want to write a guest blog? Stella welcomes drafts or suggestions for promoting your writing or thoughts there. You should be 'on topic' for her blog - see her manifesto for the topics that she covers on her blog and website. The requirements for submission are at: https://stellafosse.com/stella-fosse-author/#Submissions

ACKNOWLEDGEMENTS

It takes a village to raise a book. The village of Whixton, although imaginary, is based on places I was privileged to visit in Yorkshire, England, in March of 2023 including Dent, Grassington, and Arncliffe. There I met many friendly folks who were happy to share their history.

Special thanks to David and Mark, proprietors of the incredible Hurstwood Hall in Lancashire, who showed us the intersecting triangles carved into the stone doorway of their sixteenth century Jacobean home to ward off witches.

And I want to thank Stephanie Shields, the author of *Strange Woman*. I bought her novel about a medieval healer at a small bookstore in Grassington and was inspired by her tale of accused witches held at the Assizes in York.

Many wonderful and skilled pairs of eyes looked at this manuscript in its Beta incarnation. Margo Arrowsmith, Joann Haggarty, Sue Kamlet, Mirinda Kossoff, Jill Laing, Steeviejane Parks, Danielle Paquette-Harvey, Diana Wilde, and Becki Wright all took time from their busy schedules to read and comment upon an early version of this work. Their feedback was incredibly valuable. And particular thanks to Judith Stanton and Salem Macknee, whose eagle eyes caught many imperfections at the proofreading stage. Everyone's contributions to the finished story are so much appreciated.

The science of blood transfusions was another essential element as I wrote this time-bending story. Friends and mentors guided my way through my decades working in biologics, including blood bankers and

FDA reviewers too many to name. Everything I learned from you was important. Thanks to you all.

The suggestion to write a lesbian vampire romance came from my daughter Wynnie. I was instantly taken with this imaginative way to evoke the strength and complexity of older women—including a woman with half a millennium under her belt. "Never Too Old" takes on a whole new meaning when writing about immortals.

And many thanks to my publisher, publicist and partner for his constant encouragement and delightful company.

Historical and technical inaccuracies in this novel are mine alone. Wherever the book is authentic, it is thanks to the help I've received. For all of you who provided guidance, whether named here or not, please know that you are appreciated.

Stella Fosse

Chapel Hill, North Carolina

2023

Stella Fosse

Stella Fosse is the *nom de plume* of a sixty-something author who writes sexy stories as a creative antidote to the ageism and sexism older women face in society. She champions older women's creativity by leading workshops in seasoned romance, erotica, and memoir writing.

Stella is a frequent guest on podcasts for women past midlife. She has been published in many online venues, including *CrunchyTales Magazine*. Stella blogs about issues of interest to Women of a Certain Age, including creativity, romance, and older women's health.

Traditionally published works include her book *Aphrodite's Pen: The Power of Writing Erotica after Midlife*. Stella's story collection, *The Erotic Pandemic Ball*, is an imaginative exploration of romance in quarantine. Her first novel, *Brilliant Charming Bastard*, is a nerdy, romantic escapade through the San Francisco biotech scene. Her new book, *Vampires of a Certain Age*, expands her exploration of the vivid lives of older women.

Stella hails from California and shares the joy and empowerment of writing past midlife with women in her adopted state of North Carolina. She enjoys gathering online with women all over the world to write and laugh together.

Stella's books are available at your local bookseller and your favorite online place.

She shares her writing, as well as ideas and resources for empowering women past midlife, at www.stellafosse.com. You can also find Stella Fosse on:

Facebook: facebook.com/StellaFosseAuthor

Instagram: instagram.com/stella.fosse

Twitter: twitter.com/stellafosse

LinkedIn: linkedin.com/in/StellaFosse

—Please join her there.

ALSO BY STELLA FOSSE

Brilliant Charming Bastard

[https://books.stellafosse.com/lxhhm0146s]

Her Poly Pod: A Love in Lockdown Story

[https://books.stellafosse.com/rgi7guggfr]

Dance Macabre: A Love in Lockdown Story

[https://books.stellafosse.com/7dm2uh2yki]

The Erotic Pandemic Ball

https://books.stellafosse.com/lwnnhka5hm

Aphrodite's Pen:

The Power of Writing Erotica After Midlife

[https://books.stellafosse.com/8m3bi2ibu3]

FREE 10 Day Class: Write Your Erotic Journey through the Decades of Life

[https://page.stellafosse.com/journey]

Create a Sexy Story with Stella A FREE Seven Day Writing Course

[https://page.stellafosse.com/news_write]

AUTHOR'S NOTE

Writers are told to write what we know, and who could do otherwise? All fiction is, in a sense, autofiction: crafted from the ingredients of our lives, tossed in a blender called imagination and served up hot to our readers. Which is not to say that in writing a vampire novel I had any special knowledge of the undead; rather that living a long life (nearly twice as long as the 35-year lifespan in medieval England) has given me a taste of what it's like to "bury your friends the way most people bury their beagles," as Marion Chase uncharitably put it.

Living a long life gives older writers more grist for the mill: More people and places to carry in our hearts and share in our work. Here are some of mine.

Yorkshire, England

As a California girl, surrounded by ticky-tacky with no history, I was drawn to the handful of buildings in town that were older than the 1940s. In high school I discovered Auden and loved his sly poem, "Roman Wall Blues," but had no idea why a man in Northern England would write about such things.

In my sixties I fell in love with a Yorkshireman and traveled to York, where I walked the top of the Roman wall encircling the town. I visited the basement of the Minster, where Norman pillars of the original church stand next to remnants of the old Roman fort. In the stone village of Dent we saw the grave of a vampire from the 1500s, with its gravestone conveniently flat to the ground to accommodate a hole drilled for a spike through the heart.

Yorkshire is green and lovely and wild, a place of long history. The 1500s were a time of witch trials at the Assizes in York, while out in the country sheep farmers were cutting down the forests and killing the last of the wolves. It is a place where history is real and the dead are real.

And it is the place where Mother Shipton emerged from a tragic childhood to become the prophetess who foretold, among many other things, the Great Fire of London and the Spanish Armada.

For readers interested in learning more about Yorkshire, I recommend reading:

The History of York from Earliest Times to the Year 2000 by Patrick Nuttgens. Blackthorn Press, 2007.

Zion, Illinois

We take for granted the parents we are given—or at least, I did. When I was a child, my father's 1930s upbringing in a flat earth, faith healing cult seemed commonplace, and the stories he shared meant more to him than to me. Years after his death I realized how extraordinary his childhood had been, and began to read everything I could about his hometown of Zion, Illinois. In my early sixties I walked the streets of Zion, places with names like Ezekiel Avenue and Calgary Lane, and toured the mansion where the Reverend John Dowie lived while his congregants shivered in tents. The mansion, Shiloh House, is now a museum. There a glass case displays crutches and canes that were rescued from the Tabernacle when a disaffected congregant burned the massive building to the ground. The docent described the crutches in hushed tones as castoffs of the cured, evidence of Reverend Dowie's healing hands. But I knew from my father that these artifacts were the spoils of Dowie's trips to the pawnshops of Chicago to grace the entry of the Tabernacle on opening day.

There is more to be said about Zion than appears in this book. I am convinced that if Neil Gaiman knew what I know about the city, the final battle in *American Gods* would be set in Zion, Illinois.

For readers interested in learning more about the city of Zion, and in particular its transition from theocracy to civil government, I recommend reading:

Battle for the Garden City: Zion, Illinois, in the Twentieth Century by Jan Jansen. My Sister Publishing Company, 2011.

The Blood Banking Industry

I spent my career as a technical writer in the biologics industry, working for companies that made tests of blood safety. We always played catchup as new diseases arose. For example, in the early 1980s, when it was not yet clear that HIV was transmitted by blood, more than half the people with hemophilia in the United States contracted AIDS from contaminated clotting factors derived from blood, and many of them died.

Much like encountering a vampire, receiving blood products is risky but could also provide new life. The life expectancy of a person with hemophilia, which doubled when clotting factors were developed, plummeted with the onset of AIDS and then rose again once researchers developed ways to sterilize the clotting factors so that they could not transmit HIV. As Marion says, blood transfusions at their best really are "the magic of transferring life from person to person." And who better than a medieval healer turned vampire to appreciate that magic?

And how fortuitous that the first blood bank was in Chicago, and run by a woman—who may or may not have been Marion Chase.

For readers interested in learning more, I recommend reading:

Blood: An Epic History of Medicine and Commerce by Douglas Starr. Alfred A. Knopf, 1998.

During my career in biotechnology, I often thought about the role that herbal healers played in the history of pharmaceuticals. As maligned as those early healers have been, as witches and as quacks, the pharma industry still sends expeditions into remote areas to seek out obscure plants and bring them back to study their uses in healing. While medieval doctors relied on bloodletting, which in almost every case did more harm than good, herbal healers pioneered methods and discovered remedies that are still in use today. It has been my pleasure to touch upon this facet of women's history.

PLEASE REVIEW THIS BOOK

A Review is one of the biggest favors you can do for an author—especially on the larger vendors' sites.

Reviews are the lifeblood of writers because they let other readers—and potential readers—know what you thought of their work. Some topics to consider:

What struck you about this book?

What did you think of the storylines?

What was your opinion of the writing?

How about the editing?

What do you want to say about this book to other readers?

Please write an honest review on whichever web platform you prefer. Stella is on all the major platforms and you know *your* favorites! Stella is also on Goodreads & BookBub.

DISCUSSION GUIDE

Here are some questions to consider as you reflect on this book and discuss it with friends and in reading groups:

1. What philosophy and values do you see in this book, regarding religion and science, truth and falsehoods, youth and age, time and mortality?

2. *Vampires of a Certain Age* is a gothic romance. If you have read other books in that genre, how did this book fulfill or deviate from your expectations for the genre?

3. What surprised you about this story?

4. How did the main settings in the novel—Whixton, Zion, and the Lake County Blood Bank—affect the development of the story?

5. Unlike mortal Women of a Certain Age, Marion Chase strives to look older to avoid arousing suspicion. Is that better or worse than social pressures to look young? Why?

6. If you are a woman past midlife, are there ways you identify with Marion? For example, have you reached the point where many people you meet remind you of someone you knew before?

7. If you were writing a sequel to this book, which would you explore:

- a. Vivienne's origins in the 1400s and her adventures rescuing women through the centuries
- b. Sybil's escapades as a master barber surgeon and bloodletter
- c. How the mysterious Kate came to be a major philanthropist
- d. Sarah's life as a bawd in a Parisian brothel
- e. Rachel's research into vampire biology

8. What do you see as the major themes of this book? How well did the author explore them?

9. Did any part of this book make you feel uncomfortable? Which parts and why?

10. If you were in Marion's place, at the end of the story would you have preferred to join Vivienne and push back on government repression of women, or would you rather start the new research institute with Rachel?

11. If you could ask the author one question about this book, what would it be?

12. What was your favorite quote from the book, and why?

13. How did the author explore various forms of healing, including herbal medicine, bloodletting, blood transfusions, and even becoming a vampire?

14. This author frequently writes about the vivid lives (and love lives) of women past midlife at www.stellafosse.com. How did a vampire character of over 500 years of age help explore that idea?